LOOK BACK, MOSS

LOOK BACK, MOSS

A NOVEL BY
BETTY LEVIN

Greenwillow Books, New York

Printed in the United States of America
First Edition
10 9 8 7 6 5 4 3 2 1

Library of Congress Cataloging-in-Publication Data
Levin, Betty.
    Look back, Moss / by Betty Levin.
        p.   cm.
    Summary: Jody's involvement in his mother's
animal rescues takes on a new meaning for him
when he helps save Moss, a sheep dog that
has been mauled by a coyote after a botched
"rescue" attempt.
    ISBN 0-688-15696-7
    [1. Sheep dogs—Fiction.   2. Dogs—Fiction.
3. Animal rights activists—Fiction.
4. Animals—Treatment—Fiction.]
I. Title.   PZ7.L5759Lo   1998
[Fic]—dc21
97-34510   CIP   AC

For Susan Cooper

LOOK
BACK,
MOSS

ırday. Please, Jody willed the security officer, turn around,
back inside. Then Mom's car pulled up beside him.

Hurry!" she ordered. "Move."

ɔdy lurched toward her.

Walk!" Aunt Marie told him. "Look normal."

[e clambered into the back, where a small, white, wet-tongued
dle greeted him with ecstasy. He tried to push it away.

unt Marie said, "See how happy she is to have a friend?"

ɔdy's mother said, "Can you believe what she's been
ugh?"

ɔdy couldn't. Aunt Marie, who had spotted the car with the
dog often enough to count on its presence this Saturday,
red that the dog's owner worked inside the mall. Jody under-
d that cars heated up, even in April, even if the sunroof was
ked open. Some of the animals Mom and Aunt Marie rescued
really in a bad way and needed nursing care and medicine.
wiggly white creature didn't show any signs of heat stress,
Mom and Aunt Marie said it was always neglectful and danger-
to leave a pet locked in a car all day long.

hen they got home, Aunt Marie took the dog into her side
e house. Mom and Jody entered their side, with Mom stop-
to greet one cat after another, all of them rescued, most of
waiting for adoption.

When do we eat?" Jody asked.

ɔm said first off she had to check out the little dog. She
red up her medical bag full of discarded equipment from
et's office where she worked as a receptionist.

ly had seen her using some of those instruments to jimmy
on one of her rescue missions. Aunt Marie used standard
to pry open windows. She had taken lessons from an expert,

Sa
gc

po

th

litt
fig
stc
cr:
we
Tl
bu
ou

of
pi:
th

ga
th

a l
wi

1 Jody ducked behind a panel
being seen like this by kids fr
he minded being caught in the act. Other
Otherwise no one would notice him anyway

Mom and Aunt Marie and their friends ca
Jody couldn't help thinking of it as a steako
after the rescue was successfully completed,
would they eat.

Food smells from take-out pizzas and b
wafted over the parking lot. At least he w
entrance today. The aroma of cinnamon and
would have driven him crazy. Maybe Mom :
caught on about this and placed him strateg
tractions. Or maybe this was simply where th
be most useful.

If he caught sight of anyone who fitted th
car's owner, he was supposed to create a dive
had to be diverted, too. So far Jody had gc
twice on suspicion of shoplifting to allow M
enough time to break into a car to rescue a

Jody had given up arguing that they w
accomplice to a crime. It never got him off
Aunt Marie believed that some acts of consci
infractions of the law. Think of the greater gc
of the helpless animals they could save.

Jody eyed a security officer just emerging fr
What was taking Mom and Aunt Marie so
officer stopped and glanced at his watch. Joc
left. It seemed that his entire school was h;

a boyfriend who worked in a garage and did a lot of road service calls, including lockouts.

Sometimes Jody tried to imagine what it would be like if they were arrested. What would happen to him? Once in a while he yearned for that to happen to end the wonder and worry. But when he guessed he'd probably have to go live with his father, it usually put a stop to his yearning.

Still, the wonder drew him again and again. His mother would have to be in jail for a while. She always knew this was a possibility. But it was hard for Jody to picture what that would be like for her. Instead he imagined the police taking all the cats away. Even though one of them belonged here, Jody wouldn't let on. All the cats would go to some animal shelter, and he would have the house to himself. He'd work it out with Dad, who would give him enough money to eat out or bring meals in. Jody would take care of everything else, like laundry and cleaning the house. He'd throw out all the cat boxes. Maybe at long last the house would be rid of its zoo smell.

Mom returned, beaming, with the little white dog. She and Marie had talked it over. The dog was so small they figured she could use the backyard for a while. Later on, after the owner and the police had stopped looking for her, Jody could walk her around the neighborhood. Mom handed him the leash.

He kept his hands at his sides.

"We're giving her to you!" Mom exclaimed as the cats circled warily and hissed at the dog. "You've earned her."

Jody backed until he was against the wall. He shook his head.

"What's the matter?" Mom demanded. "Any normal kid would go wild to get their own pet."

Jody shook his head some more. A tiny white poodle? If just

one kid saw him walking it, he'd never be able to face school or the neighborhood again. "It's like for old people," he finally managed to say.

His mother made a disgusted sound. "I give up," she muttered. But halfway out the door she turned. "Still, you're going to have to help out when Marie and I are at work. You hear me, Jody?"

He nodded miserably. He supposed it would only involve taking the dog out back to pee. They wouldn't want it seen, at least for a while. "Are we going to eat soon?" he asked.

Mom said, "Marie's gone out for fried chicken. I ordered a double for you because I thought it was to celebrate." She sighed and shut the door.

Jody sat on the couch to wait for the dinner. He stared at the gray television screen, picturing on it the meal to come, the bucket of chicken, the mashed potatoes smothered in thick gravy. He clutched himself and groaned.

2 When the car horn honked, Jody's mother leaned back, glanced out the window, and remarked on a note of satisfaction that as usual Jody's father had sent his errand girl. Not Dad's errand girl, Jody corrected silently, his wife. Sharon. But Mom, who was thin and had straight brown hair, took every potshot she could at Sharon, who was big and soft and curly blond and wore gobs of dark eye makeup.

Jody was at the front door, ready to get out before Mom changed her mind and decided he was needed for another Saturday mission.

"Don't let Tina out," she called. And then, almost as an afterthought, she added, "You'd think he'd be there for you once in a while."

Jody had to open the door wide enough to drag his knapsack through. The little white dog scooted between his legs.

"Tina!" he shouted.

But the dog hadn't learned her new name yet, or else she didn't want to go back inside. She dashed toward the pickup truck and leaped, yapping, at its front wheel.

"Hey, get off that," Sharon yelled. But Tina was in a frenzy, and Sharon had to get out of the car to stop her.

"Hold her," Jody gasped. "She's not supposed to be out."

Sharon scooped up the dog, clasping her around her middle. Jody dropped his knapsack and grabbed the dog. He carried her to the house, shoved her in, and slammed the door. He was puffing as he climbed into the passenger seat beside Sharon.

"Your dad's sleeping. He had to work all night," Sharon said as they pulled away from the curb. "I've got two clients coming this morning." That's what she called her customers who came to get their hair done in her kitchen.

Relieved, Jody nodded. That meant he'd be on his own. He wouldn't have to try to shoot baskets or pitch balls. As long as Dad was asleep, Jody could even read undisturbed.

But just past noon he looked up from his book to find his father leaning against the doorjamb staring at him.

"Too good of a day to sleep through," Dad said. "I figured I'd find you here. Don't you ever move out on your own?"

Jody shut the book. He didn't even bother to make up something about doing homework. What was the point? As far as Dad was concerned, only girls read for fun and studied for school.

"Sharon says there's a new dog," Dad went on. "Stolen goods?"

Jody nodded.

"Just don't expect me to bail them out when they get caught."
Jody nodded again.

"So what are Thelma and Louise up to this weekend?" Dad
asked. "We don't want to run into them. I might have to turn
them in." Jody understood that Dad was joking now. He wasn't
about to interfere with Mom and Aunt Marie, certainly not if it
meant getting them arrested. He didn't want to have to take on
Jody full-time. Dad often said that with his extra hours, one
weekend a month was his limit.

"So do we have to steer clear of bowling, or what?" Dad
demanded.

"I think they're going to the country," Jody replied. "They
had a meeting the other night. Something about farms and cows.
No, calves. I wasn't really listening."

Dad grunted and turned into the kitchen. Jody could smell
coffee and something frying in bacon grease. He tucked his book
inside the knapsack and went to sit at the table with Dad and
Sharon.

He had to be careful now. If he showed how hungry he was,
Dad would notice and talk about making him diet. But if he
played a waiting game, eventually Sharon would let him pig out
on whatever she had fixed for Dad.

"So what's new at school?" Dad asked.

"Nothing much," Jody answered. "We're doing experiments
in science. Looking at stuff through microscopes." But that was
not what Dad was after. He wanted to hear about friends and
fooling around. Sometimes Jody made up stories ahead of time
to please him. But he could never invent them on the spot.
Instead he said, "Mom and Aunt Marie took a dog from a car

last weekend. That's why they're getting away from the scene of the crime. I helped," he added lamely.

"That little white thing?" Sharon asked.

Jody nodded.

"Looked like a spider with white fur," she commented.

"Worth a lot?" Dad asked her.

She shrugged.

Jody said, "You know they don't sell them. They never sell them. They do it for the good of the animals. To liberate them." Why did he always end up defending his mother and aunt?

Dad shoved his plate away and pushed back from the table. "Yeah . . . well . . . whatever." He wasn't interested in his ex-wife's dedication to animals. That's why he spoke of her and her sister as Thelma and Louise, two outlaws in a movie. That was how he saw them, two women flirting with trouble.

After he had shuffled off to finish dressing, Sharon heaped a plate with home fries and eggs and set it in front of Jody. "Who's going to liberate you?" she muttered as she carried Dad's empty plate to the sink.

Jody knew she didn't really expect him to answer. He dug into the food, eating steadily, silently, shoring up against the craving that plagued him wherever he was.

3 Wednesday evening seven people, all members of a group that called itself Caring About Animals That Suffer, or CAATS, met in the side of the house where Jody and his mother lived.

As long as Jody had to be pressured into helping on rescue

missions, his negative presence was not welcome at the meetings. He had no problem with that. He had managed to skim off some of the eats from the bag of munchies that Mom had picked up at the corner. He had two sci-fi books from the school library. What more could he ask for?

But it turned out that he had already read one of the books. It took about three pages before he realized this. He never read anything twice. What was the point? Once you knew the story, the book was useless. He flung it aside and opened the other one.

Excited voices intruded through the thin wall. Mom and Marie, who usually just dealt with cats and dogs, had been talking for days about what they had seen last weekend, calves in little pens with no space to run and kick up their heels. Mom was stirred up all over again as she talked about those conditions. Jody knew that CAATS had strict secrecy rules so that if any of them was arrested, the others, unconnected, could carry on their own work. So they never divulged specifics when they reported abuses or rescues, except to share information about new techniques and strategies.

Now had they moved on from cows to sheep and gorillas. No, they were discussing tactics. They must mean the other kind of guerrilla. Mom and Aunt Marie were planning some big mission. Jody couldn't tell whether it was for cows or sheep. "Please," he muttered into the pages of the book, "leave me out of it." He covered his ears with his hands.

Suddenly it came to him that there might be a way out. He would join a club at school. Even if it didn't actually do stuff on Saturdays, he could always claim that all new members had to put in extra weekend time.

He sat up straight. What if no one wanted him in their club?

Well, but weren't there other activities besides sports and the band? All he needed next time was to be too busy to chase cows or whatever it was Mom and Aunt Marie were plotting.

He rolled onto his back and stared at the ceiling. Sometimes he saw pictures there, the overhead light casting shadows into patterns that prompted stories. He thought of stampeding buffalo in westerns, hundreds of crazed beasts tumbling down a canyon and raising dust a mile high. Nimble cowboys always ducked behind boulders, but stupid villains got trampled. Movies usually showed them staring in helpless horror as the stampede bore down on them. Did Mom and Aunt Marie ever stop to consider what they might be getting into with those cows?

Tonight, though, the ceiling shadows didn't show him enough. He couldn't picture what would happen when rescuers and rescued got in each other's way. Besides, the cow patterns didn't hold their shape. All he was really able to see was a moth whacking itself to pieces against a naked lightbulb.

A light tap on his door brought him to his feet. It wasn't his mother's style when she did bother to knock. Cautiously he opened the door a crack. The little white dog squeezed through and hurled herself at him. It was almost as if she had tricked him into letting her in.

Well, two could play at that game. If he acted as though she had asked to go out, he could take her to the yard for a moment and then leave her shut in the kitchen. But this meant he had to carry her to the back door, where the leash hung on the knob. It meant going through the living room with the dog in his arms.

He hoped he could pass through unnoticed. But no such luck. Phil Kolodny, one of the two men there, called out, "Hey!" in a loud, arresting voice that brought all discussion to a halt.

"Well!" exclaimed Aunt Marie. "Bonding at last."

"She asked to go out," Jody mumbled. "I'm just taking her to pee."

His mother turned to the others. "Jody thinks he should be like his father. But he does care more than he likes to admit."

"What's wrong with caring?" Phil demanded. He was the one who had shown Mom and Marie the calves.

Jody, caught now, shook his head defensively. He didn't want to get into an argument. He didn't want to hear another lecture.

His mother said, "Jody thinks we should leave things up to the police and the Humane Society. That's what his dad tells him. Isn't that right, Jody?"

"Dad doesn't talk about it much," Jody said, thinking: Thelma and Louise.

Phil said, "The thing is, Jody, the authorities only deal with extreme cases, like using puppies to bait fighting dogs. There's always plenty of public outrage over that kind of abuse. But we're trying to raise everyone's awareness of more ordinary treatment where the feelings of animals are disregarded. Do you understand?"

Jody nodded. "That's why I'm taking this dog outside," he managed to reply as he made his escape. He stayed in the backyard longer than usual, not to show those people how caring he was but to give them time to get so absorbed again that they might not notice him slipping past them to his room without the little dog.

4 It was hopeless. Finding an extra school activity this late in the year was a bust. Maybe next fall, everyone said. Right, maybe. Jody figured he would never escape the clutches of CAATS.

Like Mom's and Aunt Marie's new big-deal mission, this time somewhere in the boonies. It had already taken a lot more planning than usual, and for the first time a third person was involved. Even though Jody did his best to ignore the whole business, he couldn't miss all the talk about optimum time slots and the need for a good-size crowd so that the rescuers could move about freely without drawing attention to themselves.

Right up until Friday night Jody kept hoping that he wouldn't be needed. After all, this time they'd have Phil along.

Then Mom informed him they were getting an early start the next morning. He should bring a toothbrush.

"Where are we going?" he asked.

"Up-country," she said. "To a trial."

His heart lifted. A trial like on television? That would be cool, or would be as long as Mom and Aunt Marie didn't cause a disturbance. Or ask him to. He supposed someone had been taken to court for animal abuse. Sometimes Mom and Aunt Marie heard about such cases and attended a trial to make sure the bad guy didn't get off.

Early Saturday morning they piled into Mom's car. Jody was a bit surprised, but not disappointed, that they left without Phil, who was stopping by later to take care of Tina. Mom drove for what seemed hours, first through the city, then on the interstate, and finally on smaller roads. Jody saw towns and mills and garages and schools and ballfields and village greens that were barely green, with houses all around them, and lumber yards and plowed fields with rows of tiny green sprouts and woodlands and pastures and hayfields still bleached from winter.

"Now, listen," Aunt Marie said to him from the front seat, "this is an altogether different kind of caper. We can't plan it in advance. Jody, are you listening?"

He said, "Yep. I thought you were planning it all week. I thought Phil was coming."

"He is," Mom said. "Later. We have to scope out the situation. We can't all be seen at the same time."

Jody began to have a sinking feeling that they were on a rescue mission after all. Maybe while he hadn't been listening, they had changed back from a court trial to cows. "I thought you already scoped out everything about those calves," he said.

"We're not doing calves," Aunt Marie told him. "The farm's too exposed. Don't you ever pay attention?"

"Jody," said Mom, "we're going to a sheepdog trial. Phil heard about it on the radio. He went to a couple of those trials last summer. They're nothing like in that movie about the pig. The dogs are miserable. The sheep are miserable. The dogs are all tied on short chains or kept in crates until they're made to chase the sheep, and the sheep run until they're ready to drop. It's no more a sport than bullfights."

"You mean, the dogs kill the sheep?" In the movie there had been some killer dogs.

"Maybe not, but it's still cruel."

Jody wondered what kinds of diversionary tactics he would have to perform. "Won't we be noticed?" he asked.

Aunt Marie shrugged. "Not if we're careful. That's where you come in. Phil says there are kids at these things. You know, like kids that are dragged along by their parents. They might be able to tell you stuff we need to know."

"So you've got to be friendly. Hang out with other kids."

Sure, thought Jody, like I'm good at that sort of thing.

"Ask questions," Mom continued. "Talk about that movie. The important thing is to separate from Marie and me. You'll just be someone there for the show."

"Here," said Marie. "Here's a sign. That must be the sheepdog trial."

Mom slowed the car. On a sweeping field that sloped up from the road a black and white Border Collie was herding five sheep between two panels. Then the dog scooted around to the side, and the sheep turned away from it and started toward a man who stood near a pen.

"The dog isn't exactly chasing them," Jody said.

"Wait," Aunt Marie replied. "Wait till you see more."

They turned off the road and drove around behind pickups and cars, campers and motor homes. Mom parked well away from the fence that separated spectators from the man and dog and sheep. "Now," she told Jody, "wander around and get a feel of things. Find out anything you can about the way this is run. Don't talk to us out here. We'll meet back inside the car around noon."

Jody looked past the many dogs and people to a refreshment table. "We didn't get breakfast," he reminded his mother.

"Oh, here," she said, thrusting a couple of dollars at him. "Buy something. Then get to work."

He nodded. Work. He might as well be a slave. She paid him with breakfast, but he had to devote his life to her cause. If he got caught doing something really illegal, he'd be in big trouble. They might really have to go to court then. Only that wouldn't be so cool, not if he was the one who ended up on trial.

5 He bought two jelly doughnuts. The first one he bit into oozed all over his fingers. He was licking them clean when he dropped the second one. Even as he stooped to retrieve it, a dog's black and white muzzle snapped it up.

"No, Moss, no!" said a girl at the other end of the dog's leash. "Sorry," she told Jody. "He's not my dog, see. He's usually good, but he's not used to me."

Jody stared at the Border Collie. The white blaze that marked the center of its face and widened at its muzzle was covered with black spots that gave it a smudged look as if it had been nosing around in ashes. The dog wagged its tail and looked expectantly with dark, intense eyes at what remained of the first jelly doughnut.

"Don't tell Janet," the girl said. "She won't let me walk him around if she finds out."

"Janet?" said Jody.

"The person he lives with," the girl told him. "Janet uses him. Trials him. He really belongs to my best friend. Only she moved away last fall. I'm here because she asked me to come see him run in a few trials."

"So why doesn't she have him?" Jody asked as he licked between his fingers and the dog strained toward him.

"Lie down, Moss," the girl ordered. She yanked the leash, and the dog dropped onto its belly, its eyes still fastened on Jody's sticky hands. "Want him to clean you off?" the girl asked. "He's good at it."

The idea of the dog's tongue all over his hands was gross. "No, thanks," he told her. "I don't need his germs."

She darted a look at him. "What germs?" Then she dropped to her knees, caught the dog's head in her hands, and kissed his spotted muzzle. "See? He's probably cleaner than that person selling you food. Dogs are naturally clean."

"Why isn't he with his owner?" Jody asked again.

This time the girl answered him. "Because he's a working dog," she said. "He was bred and trained to herd livestock. It's what he's for." She seemed to think that was all the explaining needed.

"So couldn't he do that stuff where she moved to?"

The girl shook her head. "Not in a suburb. She was totally devastated to leave him behind. But Moss belongs on a farm."

"You mean, so he can chase sheep until they drop?"

"Where do you come from?" she asked in disgust. "Where'd you pick up that kind of garbage?"

"Well, look," he declared, pointing to the field where yet another dog was bringing sheep from way back at the top end to a handler at the bottom. The sheep were running at a pretty fast clip.

"That's Janet," the girl said. "She'll get her dog, Tess, to slow the sheep."

Even as the girl spoke, the dog swung wide and then, at a sharp whistle, stopped short, letting the sheep settle. When the dog moved forward again, the sheep took off, but at a more measured pace. The dog kept sliding sideways, head held low, eyes staring to keep the sheep from bolting until finally they were guided between two gates in the center of the field.

Jody gazed in wonderment. It was as though the sheep had been transformed right before his eyes. Now the dog was in control and the sheep were somehow calmer, almost as if they trusted the dog that brought them right to that Janet person and around her and began to drive them away toward a distant set of panels halfway up the field.

Something wet brushed against Jody's fingers. Quickly he snatched his hand away from the dog's seeking tongue. To cover his reaction, he said to the girl, "Can this dog do that kind of work, too?"

The girl nodded. "Wait and see. He's not running for a while. Just listen for his name. They announce each handler and dog on the field and next in line." She told Moss to come along with her now. She told Jody that Janet wanted Moss quiet for a time before he had to run. She'd better get him hitched to the van before Janet came back from her run with Tess.

Jody took note of where the van was as he watched the girl clip a chain on to the dog's collar. The dog sat down at once, looked around, and then crawled under the van to find a bit of shade.

"He looks pretty unhappy," Jody remarked. "I bet he hates being chained up like that." He couldn't help comparing this still, silent sheepdog with Tina. The bouncy little white dog yapped and leaped for sheer joy no matter what was happening around her.

The girl sent him a look he couldn't quite decipher. "Actually," she said finally, "long ago when he was chained up all the time, he was unhappy. But that was before my friend kind of rescued him."

Rescued the dog? Did this girl belong to a family like Jody's? Were there other people this far out in the country doing Mom's kind of thing?

"This van is like a second home for Moss because it's where Janet sleeps when she stays overnight at trials. When Moss is chained here," the girl went on, "he knows it's where he belongs. And he knows his turn will come."

"His turn?" Jody repeated, trying to follow her.

"His turn to run. To work. It's what he lives for."

Jody didn't say anything more. So the girl wasn't on his side after all. That is, on Mom's side.

6   The day dragged on. Jody wandered around, trying to eavesdrop on conversations. But there were so many strange words that it was almost like listening to a foreign language. The only things that made sense to him were comments about the weather, which was unseasonably warm for early May.

By the time he went to the car to meet the others at noon he thought there was still a good chance that they would decide to look for a more crowded place to perform one of their good deeds. Even after more people came to watch the dogs herding sheep, this place was nothing like what they were used to at the mall on a Saturday, with people heading for the stores inside or else hurrying back to their cars. Here everyone stood around in small groups, looking at dogs and talking about their runs. You never knew when you came around behind a trailer or a camper whether you would stumble over a dog or a person. You couldn't really go snooping without being noticed.

Aunt Marie was the last of them to climb into the car. "So what do we know now that we didn't before?" she asked.

Mom said, "All the handlers and their families are going down the road to the grange hall for supper tonight," Mom told her. "They do that every year, and sometimes they have a meeting or dance afterward."

"Does everyone go?"

"Sounds that way," Mom answered.

"What about people like us that aren't a part of the group?"

Mom shrugged. "There's no way to tell. Some of the people here with sheepdogs just come to watch, but they like to have their dogs here with them anyway. I don't think they stay overnight. Still, we'll probably have to wait till just before dark."

Wait for what? Jody wondered. "There aren't any lights out here like in a parking lot," he pointed out.

"So it'll be dark," Mom said. "All the better." She turned to him then. "I saw you talking to a girl with a dog. Did you learn anything?"

He shook his head. "The dog belongs to someone else." He started to say that the dog's real owner lived far away, but something made him stop. The girl had been okay with him. He didn't want to focus his mom's attention on that dog.

"People talk like nothing bad happens here," Aunt Marie remarked, "but they don't notice things. They don't care that the sheep are panting after they've been run around the field."

"That place they put them in?" Mom said. "It's called an exhaust pen."

"Are we staying?" Jody asked.

"Of course we are," they both told him.

"What about lunch?" he asked.

"Here." Aunt Marie shoved a few dollar bills at him. "Go get us hamburgers."

Everything was slow. The line where he waited to place his order barely moved. It was like they'd never even heard of fast food. The church people who were grilling the hamburgers and toasting the buns seemed to know at least half the people they were serving, so there was a lot of talk and kidding around. No one seemed to mind.

"Here!" Someone nudged him with a brownie. "Here," said the girl, passing by with her lunch. "I owe you this."

"No, you don't," he replied.

"Sure I do. Moss got your doughnut. Remember?"

He remembered that Moss wasn't her dog. But he accepted the brownie. "Thanks," he said, and then asked her name.

"Diane," she told him. "What's yours?"

"Jody," he said without thinking. Maybe he should've made up a name.

She darted him one of those strange looks of hers. Guessing that she thought Jody was a girl's name, he felt himself stiffen and go red in the face. "I was named after the hero in a famous book about a boy and a deer." There, another mistake. Now she would surely remember his name later on, if whatever his mom and aunt were up to made enough of a stink to bring the police.

"What'll it be?" Somehow he had arrived at the table where orders were taken.

He glanced sideways. Diane was still within earshot, so he spoke as softly as possible. "Three hamburgers."

"Three!" Diane exclaimed.

"They're not all for me," he retorted. But he wasn't supposed to be connected with Mom and Aunt Marie. "One of them's for my dog," he blurted.

"Oh," said Diane, as if that made perfectly good sense. "I didn't know you had one."

"Not a Border Collie," he quickly replied. What if she wanted to see his dog? "Her name's Tina," he went on, prepared to admit that Tina was a sort of toy poodle cross. "I'm keeping her out of the way because she might bark and upset the working dogs. She's not trained all that well."

Diane nodded approvingly. "Janet says that some dogs in the audience that bark or snap through the fence can startle the sheep and ruin someone's run."

His three hamburgers were slapped onto paper plates and shoved to the end of the table where there was relish and ketchup. With his back to Diane, he slathered on everything available. Only when he was stacking the plates did it occur to him that Diane might wonder what kind of dog ate relish. Turning, he scanned the people on the other side of the line. Diane was nowhere in sight.

Jody heaved a huge sigh. Home free, he thought, stuffing the brownie into his mouth before hoisting the layered hamburgers and looking for a way to the car that would keep him clear of Janet's van, where he guessed Diane was heading.

7   During the early afternoon the trial seemed to go into slow motion. The sheep kept dropping their heads to look for new green shoots in turf still matted and bleached by last winter's snows. A few of the older ewes turned to face the dogs that crowded or tried to rush them. If a dog had to nip at one to force her to turn and move on, it was disqualified for what the announcer called gripping.

Just when it seemed to Jody that nothing really bad was allowed to happen on the course, one handler lost his temper at his dog, first yelling at it and then grabbing it and giving it a shake as he left the field. The dog cowered away from him and then slunk along at heel.

"Someday Billy'll go too far," a man near Jody remarked, and the person he was speaking to suggested that they keep an eye on Billy till he cooled down. The two men moved away from the fence.

"Hear that?" Diane said, stepping closer to Jody. "I've been listening to those two guys all through that run. They said that Billy Mount used to be a great handler, but he's losing his grip."

"But it was the dog that bit the sheep," Jody pointed out.

Diane said, "Those guys are handlers, too. They were saying that Billy Mount puts too much pressure on his dogs. When things go wrong, he takes it out on them."

Jody didn't know what she meant by pressure. All he said was: "You can see his dog's scared of him."

Diane nodded. "Now look over there at Moss with Janet."

It took a moment for Jody to pick out one dog and person among all the others. Janet was seated in a folding chair with Moss right against her legs. As she leaned forward to watch the dog currently fetching sheep off the hill, her hands rested on Moss's shoulders.

"You said she wanted Moss tied up before he ran," Jody reminded Diane.

"She wants him quiet," Diane explained. "Focused."

"You know a lot about all this," he said. "Can you get Moss to work, too?"

Diane shook her head. "I never tried. My friend Zanna worked hard with him all last summer. She learned a lot from Janet and Janet's grandfather, who started Moss's training and then had a stroke and couldn't work him anymore. It was Zanna's thing, not mine."

"But Moss knows you," Jody said. "He likes you."

Diane nodded. "Sort of, yes. Sometimes he looks past me, like he's waiting, like he thinks Zanna's about to show up. Maybe I remind him of her." Diane sighed. "I can't wait for her to come."

"She's coming? When's that?"

"Beginning of July. She's going to help out with Janet's kids. She and Moss will be together for the rest of the summer." Diane squinted as she gazed up the field. "I'm going to the airport to meet her when she comes. I want to bring Moss, but Janet says it's too long a trip from Coventry all the way to Bangor and back, and he'd have to stay in the van the whole time."

Jody glanced over at Janet and Moss, but they were gone, the chair empty.

"Here goes," Diane exclaimed. She was looking toward the gate as Janet walked through into the field. "I've got to pay attention to this. Zanna will want to know every single thing Moss does."

Jody wanted to pay attention, too, because this was the only competing dog he even half knew. Moss stayed behind Janet much the way Billy Mount's dog had stayed behind him. Moss didn't look exactly happy either. He carried his head low, his tail even lower. He kept tilting his muzzle from one side to the other as if he were trying to avoid bumping into the back of Janet's legs. Still, he was almost glued to her until she reached the handler's post. Then he stepped to one side and froze.

Janet gazed across the expanse to the top end of the field where a dog and handler were setting out five sheep for this run.

Jody kept his eyes on Moss. But when the dog took off, it was as if from some invisible signal. Janet hadn't moved. Neither had Moss until the instant he bounded away from her.

Jody glanced at Diane, who was clutching the fence post in front of her. "Beautiful!" she exclaimed. "Perfect outrun."

"Not perfect," a woman on the other side of her remarked. "The dog's running too wide. Out of contact."

Diane glared at her and drew closer to Jody. "Wait and see," she whispered to him. "I bet the judge thinks it's perfect."

By now Moss was behind the sheep, which headed straight for the fetch gates in the middle of the field. When the sheep started

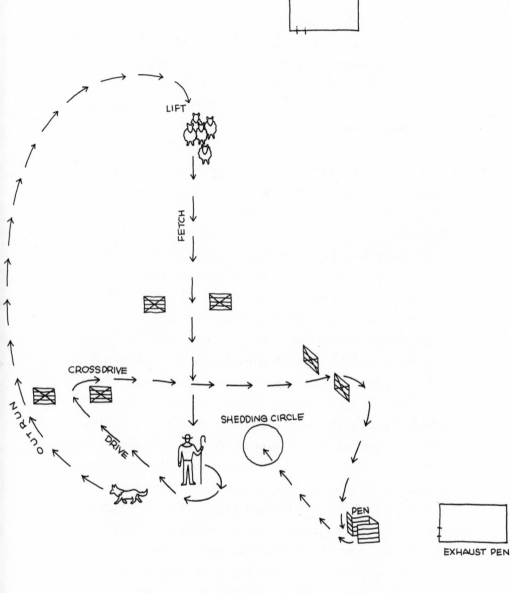

HOLDING PEN

LIFT

FETCH

CROSS DRIVE

SHEDDING CIRCLE

OUT RUN

DRIVE

PEN

EXHAUST PEN

TYPICAL SHEEPDOG TRIAL COURSE

to veer toward the exhaust pen, Janet whistled two quick notes that were a signal to Moss. He flanked around to force the sheep to straighten their direction. By the time he brought them to Janet, they were walking quietly. Still, Jody noticed that they were puffing from the exertion of the gather. "They look tired," he murmured, mostly to see what kind of reaction he'd get from Diane.

"What? Oh, the sheep." She shrugged. "Maybe a little." She was concentrating on Moss, though, as he drove the sheep toward a pair of panels that formed a gate halfway up one side of the field.

What was the point of bringing the sheep all this way and then driving them off again? Jody decided this wasn't the time to ask. Besides, an explanation would probably contain terms like *outrun* and *out of contact* that left Jody behind anyway.

Something went wrong at the gate. Jody couldn't tell what it was because it looked as though the sheep had gone through, but people in the audience groaned, and Diane said, "Oh, no!"

"What's wrong?" another onlooker asked, and the woman who had said that Moss had run too wide explained that two of the sheep had come back through the gate instead of turning past it. The judge would deduct points for that.

Meanwhile the sheep were on their way across the field, Janet quietly whistling occasional commands to Moss, who kept moving off to one side to keep them going straight as they approached the next set of panels. As the sheep went between them, Janet whistled a brief stop that kept Moss from swinging around too sharply and repeating the error at the first drive gate.

Again Jody glanced at Diane to see how she regarded the rest of Moss's run. He didn't get the part after the sheep were penned when two had to be separated from three. But the applause on this side of the fence confirmed that Janet and Moss had done well.

Without a backward glance at him, Diane tore away. A moment later he saw her walking with Janet and some other people toward the van. Jody kept his distance, but he caught a glimpse of Moss flopped down, his paws on either side of a water bowl, with Diane kneeling and speaking to him. Even while the dog lapped water, his tail brushed the ground in what seemed like a slightly reserved acceptance of her praise.

They had been waiting for him in the car. As they drove out of the parking area, Mom told him to yell good-bye to the girl he'd been talking to. He couldn't bring himself to yell, but Mom drove close enough so that he could wave out the window. Diane sort of waved back.

"You leaving before the end?" she called to him.

He nodded. He had mixed feelings about going now.

"Tell her you might be back tomorrow," Aunt Marie said to him.

He said, "I hope Moss wins something." Now that he had watched Moss's run so closely, he was ready to pay more attention to the trial. Listening to the handlers' comments might be different now. Even if he only understood a fraction of what they said, it could give him a better idea of what to look at. Besides, Diane might fill him in.

All the same, getting out of there meant leaving behind whatever scheme Mom and Aunt Marie had been cooking up. Maybe they decided they were out of their league here. It was one thing to meddle at home, where Aunt Marie could keep track of a dog for days or even weeks before they made their move, but out here they didn't know enough about the sheep or the dogs or the people.

Mom and Aunt Marie were embroiled in some ongoing argument. He didn't bother to try to clue himself in. If they were heading home, who cared whether one approach was better than another?

All things considered, he guessed he was relieved to be out of there. He began to wonder whether they would stop for supper or drive straight through.

This morning's scene passed by in reverse order: farm, farm, lumber yard, ballfield, village green, garage, farm, school. And then the car slowed and turned into a motel driveway. Why here, in the middle of nowhere? Jody could see only two cars pulled up in front of motel room doors. Then he recognized Phil's van. Did this mean they weren't done with the sheepdog trial after all?

They gave him a bag of chips and sent him into the adjoining room to watch television. The reception was lousy. It wasn't just that everything here was scuzzy, but there didn't seem to be much to look at even when the screen showed something.

He went around to the other door to see if he could find out what was going on. Tina hurled herself at him. Phil must have brought her. But why? Were they planning to stay?

"Take the dog for a walk," Aunt Marie ordered. "Out behind, where she can go. Don't let her off the leash."

The little dog danced around him, entangling his feet. What if they brought her back to the trial? He would rather die than let Diane see him like this. He would refuse. Didn't he have any rights at all?

Behind the motel the lawn suddenly dropped away into swampland. Tina was drawn in that direction. He was tempted to let her go. What was the point of rescuing her and then keeping her prisoner?

He glanced toward the row of rooms. Not one of them had a window in its back wall, so no one could see him. He might just let go of the leash for a moment and give her a taste of freedom. He gazed around. What could be the harm? Still, he hesitated. If Tina made a dash for the road and a car was coming, that would be the end of her. If she ran down to the swamp, he might have to go into that muck to drag her out.

He stood there with the little dog tugging at the end of her leash until Mom called him in.

They were going back to the trial in Phil's van. It seemed to be part of the plan they had been concocting. Mom's car, which would have been noticed, would be nowhere near the place when they rescued the sheep.

The sheep? Somehow Jody had assumed that it was some dog they suspected of being abused that they would liberate. That would be the reason why Tina had to be left for now in the motel. But the sheep? How could that be done? Where would they put them all?

 Jody peered up through the front window to see what was going on.

"You lie low," Mom told him. "This is a waiting game now. You can't be seen until tomorrow."

Their arrival was timed to coincide with as much coming and going as possible. Mostly only the audience was going, though.

Handlers and their families were in and around their campers and trucks, some feeding dogs, some letting them run.

"You said the sheep would be kept in that corner pen," Phil complained. "How can we get them if they're spread all over that field?"

Aunt Marie said, "Don't worry. It's probably like the lunch break when they let them out to graze. Someone said that the sheep would have to be closed in overnight with hay and water in what they call the exhaust pen because the fence at the back of the field is down."

"I hope you're right," Phil muttered. "We're going to have to move quickly and then get out of here fast."

"We are right," Mom said. "You'll see. Everyone will be heading for the grange hall down the road."

"Like when?" Phil demanded.

Mom shrugged. "Probably soon. Why are you so uptight about all this?"

"It's more of a risk than usual," he said.

"It was your idea in the first place," Aunt Marie reminded him.

"Jody, keep down," Mom snapped as someone walked a couple of dogs right past the van.

"They can't see through tinted windows," Jody said.

"Down," she ordered.

Everyone was tense, not just Phil. Jody was glad to be out of it.

"Why didn't you leave me back at the motel?" he asked suddenly.

Phil threw him a look and said, "We might need you to watch, to warn us if anyone's coming."

Jody didn't ask how he could do that if he had to lie low in the back of the van. Phil unwrapped a stick of gum and popped it in his mouth. "What I wouldn't give for a smoke now," he declared.

"That's why you're on edge," Mom said. "Quitting's the pits."

Phil nodded, chomping noisily.

One or two more vehicles drove out and down the road. People called, offering rides.

"God," said Aunt Marie, "if they forget to pen the sheep, we're sunk."

"No, look!" Mom exclaimed.

Jody poked his head up in time to see a dog gathering all the sheep and bringing them to the exhaust pen. There was a kind of grandeur about it, the maneuver seemingly effortless, the dog running wide and then slowing as the sheep funneled through the small gate. Jody never did see who was directing the dog. Light was leaking from the sky, drawing with it details and color. The scene might have been a movie fading from the television screen.

Even after it seemed as though everyone had left the parking area, Mom and Aunt Marie insisted on waiting. Phil argued that they needed every bit of remaining light. They disagreed. Darkness would cover them in case someone came back unexpectedly. What if one person in the house across the road had stayed at home?

When finally the front doors of the van opened and then quietly shut, Jody clambered into the front to watch.

For a long time nothing happened. He couldn't see much because of all the vehicles between the van and the exhaust pen. Suddenly the dark spaces filled with moving white blobs as sheep milled about the campers and motor homes.

Mom ran to the van and then stood beside the door without getting in. She was breathless.

"What happened?" Jody asked.

"They wouldn't come out. They didn't want to leave that pen."

"Now what?"

"Don't know," she told him. "We hoped they'd go out into that big back field, but they seem to think they're supposed to cross the road. That's where the barn is."

"Maybe they don't like being out at night," he suggested.

She drew a long breath. Then she said, "You'd better get out. We need to head them away from the road before a car comes along and hits one. Hurry, Jody."

"What do you want me to do?" he asked.

"Run at them," she said. "Clap your hands. Anything to turn them."

"Scare them? Isn't that cruel?"

"Only to save them," she gasped, running to block a few that were dashing up the incline.

"Maybe we should get help," Jody said, "someone with a dog."

"Over here," Phil shouted. He was jumping up and down and waving his arms. The sheep he turned bumped into those still coming. They circled, blatting to one another, clearly spooked by the strangers in the gloom.

Jody, still inside the van, was afraid to make things worse. What they needed was one sensible person, like Janet, who could round up these panicked animals and put them safely back inside their pen.

He was thinking about making a break for it, just running past this mess and heading for the grange hall to get help, when two dogs appeared from nowhere. For a moment they were like silhouettes against the waning light. Not Border Collies. Nothing like the Border Collies he'd been watching all day. It was impossible to tell whether they had come from the barn or house or had just been traveling along the road.

They paused for an instant. Their effect on the sheep was electrifying. The animals came from all over the parking area. They bunched up, stock-still, and faced the dogs. The sheepdogs tied to trucks and campers rose and stared, too, first at the sheep, then at the strange dogs. By now another one had appeared.

Jody heaved a sigh. He didn't have to go to the grange hall after all. Whatever kind of dogs they were, maybe some other type of sheepdog, they had come in the nick of time, not just saving the sheep but saving Jody's skin as well.

As soon as these dogs plunged down from the road, the sheep moved away from them. A few of the tied Border Collies began to growl. Probably they didn't like outsiders taking over their job.

The problem was obvious to Jody. There wasn't anyone around to give the visiting dogs orders. Or else call them off. They didn't work like Border Collies either. They stalked and then suddenly lunged.

Jody was out of the van now, but he had no idea how to fix this mess. He caught a glimpse of Aunt Marie running at a tangle of dog and sheep. She shrieked as she flung her arms at them. He had no idea where his mother was, but he saw Phil dragging the gate wide and shouting something. Was he trying to call the sheep back into the pen?

Those that actually heard him and saw the gate darted toward safety, one of the dogs in hot pursuit. Others just scrambled any which way until they reached a dirt track that led to another field beyond the trial course. Jody remembered that the field was vast and bordered by woods. The dim light gave it a flattened look, like open water. The sheep that scattered over its pale light surface seemed to bob as if they were partly swimming, partly drowning.

One growling Border Collie began a kind of moan. It thrust its muzzle skyward and began to howl. Within seconds the howling spread to others. The clamor was so tremendous that it dragged Jody's attention away from the chase. There was Moss and Janet's dog, Tess, both straining away from the van, sounding crazed and unreachable.

He didn't dare approach them. He didn't know what could be done to restore Moss to being the dog that had swiped his doughnut and offered Diane a modest wag of his tail.

10 The first people to appear along the road were on foot and so breathless they could barely speak. One of them was Diane. Another was Jody's mother, who veered away from the others as they dashed into the parking area.

Running to meet them, Aunt Marie shouted and pointed toward the trial course and the back field. Then she caught sight of Mom and ducked around behind them. "You went to the grange?" she exclaimed.

"Get in the van," Mom gasped.

"What difference does it make?" Aunt Marie began to argue. "If they saw you—"

"Inside!" Mom hauled herself up by the steering wheel, but Marie took off again.

By now pickups and cars were heading down from the road. In an instant the howling stopped, replaced by shouts that passed between the running figures.

A shot was fired on the trial course. A terrible yelping that was almost a human scream was silenced by a second shot. Now Phil came racing toward his van. He halted, pointing the way Aunt Marie had. Jody guessed he was telling people that some of the sheep had escaped into the back field. In all the mingled voices it was impossible to make out more than an occasional word or phrase. But Jody was almost certain that he saw Diane unhitch Moss from Janet's van.

He wanted to stay. He wanted to find out what was going on and how everything would end. But Phil said that was out of the question. He was furious because Marie was still outside where she might be recognized and because they ought to get out while the going was good.

"Maybe I should be in that field with her," Mom said. She sounded angry, too, but in a different way. "They might need help with injured animals."

"They'll get a vet," Phil told her. "Besides, farmers know how to take care of their animals."

"Not like this," Mom said, her words choked. "Anyway, they saw me at the grange hall."

Phil snapped at her. "You know we could get caught here. You risked more than this one mission. Besides, it wasn't necessary; all the howling would have alerted these people."

Another shot was fired. Mom said, "I had to do something. Everything was happening so fast. You couldn't stop those dogs. I couldn't stop them. Something had to be done. The sheep were terrified." Two more shots followed.

Phil said, "I'm going to look for Marie." He left the van door open.

Jody strained to make sense of what he could hear from voices nearby. Someone was trying to describe the land beyond the field. Someone else was urging caution. "You send too many dogs after them sheep, and they'll be all over creation."

"That's right," another agreed. "Sheep spook so bad in the dark you can't hardly hold them."

"Daylight," a new voice suggested. "Anything else now will only make matters worse."

"That's right," repeated the agreeing voice. "It's like serving them up to the coyotes."

Coyotes? Jody was baffled.

Aunt Marie, in tears, lashed out at Phil as he hustled her into the van. "This is your idea of outreach?" she demanded.

"What's the matter with you and Brenda? You can't fall apart every time things don't work out just like we planned. It's not my fault those dogs showed up."

"Coyotes," Aunt Marie told him. "At least that's what they're saying about the one they shot."

"Coyotes!" Phil exclaimed. "I never thought—"

"What were the other shots?" Mom asked.

"Sheep," Aunt Marie told her. "They're killing the ones that are torn up. Not even trying to save them."

"That doesn't surprise me," Phil responded. "It's more proof that they don't care about the animals they use. I wish it didn't turn out like this, but we were right to stop the sheepdog trial."

Mom shook her head. "Maybe," she said, "maybe not. Let's go home."

Phil started up the van, and they pulled out onto the road.

"I don't think anyone connected us at all," Phil remarked. "When we come in the morning, you'd better be in your own car again."

"No," Mom told him. "We should go home."

"No way," he said. "You and Marie and Jody need to show up just like you expect everything to go on."

Aunt Marie turned to Jody's mother. "Phil's right. Just because something went wrong doesn't mean what we tried to do was wrong. We've got to see this through."

Jody's mother didn't answer.

"Except, Brenda," Phil added after a moment's thought, "you shouldn't've gone to the grange hall without asking or telling us. That's not playing by the rules."

"So what?" Mom retorted. "So they'll think I was someone who happened to drive by and noticed there was trouble. It was natural to go to the one place nearby that was all lit up. Anyone would if they saw—" She broke off, shuddering.

"You were reacting, not thinking."

"I was trying to save the sheep."

On went the talk. Jody stopped listening.

When finally Phil pulled over at a convenience store gas station, everyone got out to use the toilet and pick up something to eat. Since the store was about to close, and the counterwoman expected an early-morning delivery, she let Jody take the last cut pizza slices for the price of one. He loaded up on Danish, too.

In the dark of the van, with the grown-ups still going over the day's events, he stuffed himself without paying attention to which food came first. It was all the same to him, sweet or tangy, just so long as it filled him up. When he ate like this, he tended to shut out the world. He knew that Mom and Aunt Marie and Phil were worked up over the failed rescue, but he didn't bother to listen to where the blames was cast or what, if anything, could be done about it.

It was only when he was finished and wiping his sticky fingers on his pants that he felt a sharp tug of memory like the flick of a dog's warm wet tongue. Diane's words came back to him then: "Want him to clean you off? He's good at it."

Good at more than that, thought Jody. He pictured the dog out in the field taking the sheep around the course. Jody was almost glad they'd be back tomorrow. He wanted to see Moss run again. He wanted to see Diane.

11 Even though they checked out of the motel, Phil left his van there. That meant they had to bring Tina with them. Jody cringed at the thought of being made to take her out on a leash in front of all those sheepdog people. But then he remembered that he had mentioned her to Diane. If Tina were seen with him and then with his mom, that could blow their cover. A small white dog, which was likely to draw some notice, could link them.

Since when had he started thinking this way? Mom's way. Was this how the criminal mind worked, always alert to hazards, weighing the odds? His fantasy about his mom and his aunt's being exposed could actually happen. That would put an end to their rescue missions. What a relief it would be! Except that the next stage, where he would be more or less left to his own devices, was more like a dream. They didn't let you be alone really. A kid he knew of was in foster care because his parents got into trouble.

Jody was so engrossed in these thoughts that he didn't realize they had arrived until the car drove down the slope into the parking area. As far as he could tell, everything looked like yesterday, except that it was too early for much of an audience to have gathered.

"I can't believe it!" Aunt Marie exclaimed. "It's like nothing happened. What's with these people? Are they monsters?"

"Cool it," Phil told her. "Someone might hear you."

"Well, it's disgusting. They're making sheep run over the blood of sheep that died out there last night."

Jody's mother tied a scarf over her head. She said, "Looks like rain." Then she turned to Jody. "We're not staying long, so make the best of it."

Make the best of what? he wondered.

"Just keep your distance from us until it's time to go," Aunt Marie told him. "Then come to the car like before."

He almost got away without Tina. Almost, but not quite. Phil caught up with him and thrust the little white dog at Jody before he could pretend not to hear or see. Jody glanced around the area. People were either absorbed in the run on the trial course or talking together in subdued but intense voices. Short of pushing his way into their midst, there was no way for Jody to pick up anything they were saying.

He wondered where Diane was, since neither she nor the dogs were at Janet's van. At least she wouldn't see him with Tina. Not that it mattered, since she already knew he had a small, useless dog.

Dragging Tina along, he went to look at the order of running posted on a sheet of cardboard with scores written in beside the names of dogs that had already run. Moss was up soon. Maybe Janet and Diane had taken the dogs for a walk in the back field.

Jody took off for the gap that led to that field. Except for a backhoe beside some mounds of raw earth nearby, the field looked empty. He went back to Janet's van and called into it. Diane and Janet must have spent the night there. Maybe Diane was sleeping in because they had been up so late on account of the disaster with the sheep. There was no answer, no sign of life.

Jody went to watch the trial. At least he would be there when Janet walked out to the handler's post with Moss. He listened carefully each time the announcer called a name and alerted the next person in line to run. But when Janet's name came up, it was only to remind the handler after her to be ready to take her place.

"What's happened?" Jody asked the man standing beside him. "Where's Janet?"

"Looking for the dog. Some didn't come back. They brought one in early this morning, all tore up. They went off again, just a few of them."

"But why didn't the dogs come back?" Jody asked. "Were they lost?"

The man looked at Jody. "Some stood by the sheep. Some of them sheep was run into the river. Coyotes got them there." The man turned away. It was clear that he didn't want to talk about it anymore.

But what did he mean? Got who?

Jody wandered along the fence, stopping when he thought people were talking about what had happened.

"What difference does it make whether they're coyotes or coydogs?" one woman argued with another. She snapped her fingers at the Border Collie beside her, and it dropped to its belly, its eyes fastened on the sheep on the trial course. "There can't be many pure coyotes anywhere these days. Most are part dog."

"Still," said her companion, "if we had stricter laws, there'd be fewer dogs loose to add to the problem."

Jody had never heard of a coydog, but it wasn't hard to figure out that it was a combination of a dog and a coyote. So were those dogs that came across the road last night that kind of mix? Jody tried to recall what they were like. In the twilight they had looked ordinary, that's all. The thing he remembered was how the sheep reacted. They had seemed to sense that the dogs off the road, or what he had taken for dogs, were dangerous. The sheep had been terrified, instantly aware that they were not about to be herded.

Jody was watching the trial without really seeing it. Instead he was trying to picture Diane running, running. He was trying to place her in all that confusion. Had Moss been with her, or had Jody just imagined that he was?

A couple, newly arrived, squeezed in between Jody and the two women and asked what was going on. They were told that because some sheep had been attacked and killed, each competing dog was running only three ewes today instead of five. These remaining sheep were hard to handle, unpredictable. Still, what could you do but make the best of it?

Jody was so used to his mother's and aunt's convictions on animal matters that it came as a surprise that there could be other positions not entirely different and yet not the same. It occurred to him that Mom and Aunt Marie were probably hearing this kind of talk, too. It must just about kill them to keep their mouths shut.

Jody sensed a shift in focus on this side of the fence before he caught on to what was happening. People were turning from the trial course, some of them moving toward the back field. He followed, but he was slow to discover what they were looking at. Then he caught sight of the tractor. It seemed to be inching along a dirt track that skirted the edge of the woods on the far side of the back field. At first he couldn't make out what it was hauling. Then he saw several figures sitting at the rear of the flatbed trailer hitched to the tractor.

More people came to stand in the gap between the fields. They waited without speaking to one another. In the silence Jody could hear the clear whistles of the handler back on the trial course. Yet it seemed to him that almost everyone was here watching the tractor approach.

Time was suspended. A pair of red-tailed hawks soared above the field and were driven off by a mob of frenzied crows. The sun, no more than a yellow stain in the overcast sky, gave the birds the look of cutout figures. Nothing was quite real until the tractor roared in and stopped, idling beside the backhoe. The people on the flatbed jumped down.

One of them carried a dog. Jody recognized the man. He was Billy Mount. No one spoke to him as he walked to the edge of the turned soil and dropped the dog into what Jody now realized was a hole in the ground. No one spoke to him as he turned away, his arms extended as though he could still feel the weight of his dog in them.

Wait a minute, Jody wanted to say. Wasn't this the man with the temper, the man who was mean to his dog yesterday?

Jody looked around at the people who stood aside as Billy Mount walked off from them and kept on walking toward his truck.

Meanwhile sheep were hauled off the flatbed, dragged a few yards, and dumped into the hole. The dead animals looked like balloon figures with enormous bellies and stick legs that waved as if they still possessed some vestige of life.

"How many in this lot?" called the handler who had just run his dog.

"Nine," answered a woman who had helped roll another animal into the hole. Jody recognized her at once. She was Janet. Then, looking for Diane, he found her standing off to the side of the trailer, Tess panting at her feet.

Even though Diane was wearing the same clothes as yesterday, he barely recognized her. Her light brown hair looked stringy today and longer. Or was it that she seemed to have shrunk? Her bangs were all over her eyes, her face almost hidden.

"No sign of Moss?" one of the watchers who had been standing there finally asked.

Janet shook her head.

"That's good," someone said in an encouraging tone. "He's made it then. He'll find his way back."

Janet nodded. She walked stiffly, like a person on guard. Beckoning to Diane, she headed for the parking area.

12

The others were already in the car when Jody climbed in back. Phil, recoiling, told him to take it easy and stay on his side. Look how he was getting everything wet.

"Why did you stay out so long?" his mother asked him.

Jody didn't answer. Even after it had started to rain, he had hung around Janet's van waiting to talk to Diane. But the only time she had appeared Janet was with her. They had walked together to the Porta-John, which didn't seem the right place to approach. Besides, Diane wasn't alone long enough to allow him to ease into conversation with her.

He blew on his hands to get the rawness out of them and tried to keep his bulky self apart from Phil.

Aunt Marie said, "I think we should leave flyers anyway." This was obviously a discussion already under way. "Otherwise no one's going to make the connection between how they're abusing those animals and what they suppose is just bad luck."

"I heard someone wondering how the gate was left open in the first place," Mom said. "Maybe they need time to deal with this crisis."

"But they're not really dealing with it," Phil told her. "They're just going ahead like nothing happened. I mean, except someone like the guy with the dead dog."

"Don't feel too sorry for him," Aunt Marie retorted. "I've heard he didn't even try to save his dog. He just shot it."

"Wait a minute," Mom objected. "Everyone says the dog was barely alive when they found it. Much worse off than the dog that was taken to a vet early this morning."

"But how could he shoot his own dog?" Aunt Marie demanded.

Jody saw again the man dropping his dog into the burial pit along with the savaged sheep, saw him walking off with his arms out in the carrying position, empty.

"The poor dog's probably better off," Phil muttered. "His life must've been a living hell."

"I suppose some of them are kind to the dogs. You can see that. But the ones that sound so mean, what makes their dogs keep on until . . ." Mom's voice fell away.

Aunt Marie broke in with renewed conviction. "They ought

to know that we were making a statement here. They need to be shaken up."

"But that'll finish us here," Phil pointed out.

"The next sheepdog trials are in other places," she argued.

"But wherever they are, these people will be looking for us. I think we should get out now and plan another liberation mission for later on." He turned toward Mom, who was now sitting behind the wheel. "What do you think, Brenda?"

Mom swiveled, dislodging the little white dog lying between her and Aunt Marie. She shook her head. "I don't know," she said. "I don't know what I think. I guess," she added after a pause, "I don't ever want to come to another one of these things."

"But you want them to be stopped, don't you?"

Mom nodded. Her voice dropped. "Maybe we should stick to what we know."

Phil made a disgusted sound.

Aunt Marie said, "You give up too easily."

Mom didn't answer. The rain had stopped pinging on the roof of the car. All at once Jody realized that the racket made by the backhoe was over, too. A piercing whistle could be heard from the trial course. He felt enclosed and almost warm now. He had no desire to leave the comfort of the car.

"You know things can go wrong at home, too." Marie picked up the little dog and settled her on her lap. "What if I'd been arrested rescuing Tina? What if Jody had to make a diversion and got picked up by security again? Would you have quit?"

Mom shook her head. "No." She sounded weary, defeated.

"You just feel bad about the losses," Phil said consolingly. "You mind the suffering."

"I mind that we let it happen," she answered, "that we didn't know what we were doing."

"I mind that, too," Phil told her. "Next time we'll do it differently. So let's get out of here now while we're still unnoticed."

Marie said, "Tina needs to go out first. Jody, can you take her for a pee?"

Jody pressed back into the corner. Why him? Tina wasn't his responsibility.

"Go on," Aunt Marie urged, opening her door. "Look, it's not even raining anymore. Give the love a little walk."

Heaving himself forward, Jody got out and went around to receive Tina's leash. "How long?" he asked.

"A little while. We need to get some information on the next scheduled trials. Be back here by the time they break for lunch, and you can pick up something for us all."

Lunch. He hadn't thought about food until she mentioned it. Now hunger clenched him. Even walking in the opposite direction from the church booth didn't help. The aroma of grilled hot dogs and hamburgers followed him out through the gap into the back field.

Drawn to the burial hole, he approached its edge and looked down. Even though it wasn't filled, he could see nothing but loose subsoil. Did he imagine a faint smell of death? Just knowing that beneath the subsoil lay slaughtered sheep and a dog gave him a sour taste in his mouth.

Tina, nosing at a pile of rubble, began to dig furiously, her muzzle and paws sticky with muck. To his horror he realized that she had discovered some blood. It hadn't occurred to him that it must have dripped from the sheep as they were dragged from the trailer. He yanked her away from the mess. He didn't dare take her to the car like that. Where could he find some water?

Back in the parking area he saw that every truck or car with dogs tied to it had water dishes. Where did the water come from? Then he saw the jugs and cans on tailgates or on the ground. If people had brought their own water, he couldn't exactly borrow some when he had no way to return it.

"Is there any water?" he asked a handler setting out for the trial field with a dog.

The handler glanced down at Tina and grinned. "Looks like you need more than I can spare. You better get that pup down to the river. Follow the tractor tracks. Go along the edge of the field and then through the woods." He seemed anxious to get going. "But keep that little dog leashed. Coyotes out there would snap it up before you could blink."

Unsure about going that far, Jody watched the handler stride toward the gate to the trial field with his eager Border Collie prancing in circles around him.

Jody considered returning to the car. But the thought of Phil, who couldn't stand being close to one wet person, presented with a soaked, grimy dog was enough to send Jody in the other direction. Along the tractor tracks. Into the woods. Toward the river.

13 Trudging through the woods, Jody was certain that he had missed a turn. Paths that branched off the main track just petered out. Every time he came to a stack of timber or a heap of stones he thought he must have reached some kind of destination. But there was no river, no sound of water. Of course there were lots of birdcalls. Maybe they prevented his hearing anything else.

Tina began to balk. Twice she sat down, once belly-flopping into a mud puddle. He pulled her up sharply. That was all he needed, he thought. What if he had to carry her with all that mud and gore on her? That would really give Phil something to complain about.

When he heard a call, at first he thought it was some bird. Then the call became a word, and the word was *Moss*. He stopped to listen. The call came again: "Moss! Mossie!" The voice wavered on one sustained, plaintive note. "Mossss!"

"Diane?" he shouted.

The calling broke off. And then: "Who's there?"

"Jody," he answered. "Where are you?"

"Here," she said, sounding desolate. "Nowhere."

"Wait up," he said, dragging the little dog after him through the underbrush. She kept getting tangled around twigs and roots. "Diane!" he yelled again, afraid that he had lost her.

She stomped toward him, soaked and bedraggled. "Jody," she said. She saw Tina. "Well, so that's your dog." Then she asked, "What are you doing here?"

"Looking for the river. I've got to wash her off."

"I'll show you. Over here," she told him. "I'm beginning to know my way around. But if we get Moss back safe and sound, I'll never come here again. Never."

He followed her until finally they were on a path that rounded a giant boulder. "Moss," she called as she pushed branches aside. "Mossie!" She pointed ahead. "Just down there," she told Jody. "It's pretty shallow, but there's plenty of water for bathing any-thing that small."

The woods thinned as they approached the bank. Jody felt a trace of warmth from the sun he could no longer see. The water skirted logjams. It tumbled over falls that flattened abruptly, swirling and then leveling off until the next dam dashed it downward again. Birds dipped into the spray and shot skyward, flicking droplets like iridescent marbles in the air.

"Is this where the sheep were?" Jody asked. "Did you see them here?"

Diane shook her head. "They were upriver. The coyotes drove them into deeper water where they couldn't cross, couldn't stand. The second bunch were over there. That's where we found the dog, too."

"But not Moss," he said.

"Not Moss."

He knew he should say something hopeful. He tried to recall what people had said to Janet.

Diane said, "I can help you with your dog if we hurry. I need to keep moving in case Moss is somewhere and can't stand or walk."

"That's okay," he said, pulling Tina down to the water's edge. Diane came with him, though. She picked Tina up under the belly and waded out into the swifter water. Tina flailed and then yelped hysterically as Diane dunked her. Plunging into the river to catch up, Jody gasped. He scrubbed and splashed the little dog, while Diane tipped the mucky muzzle to wash it off.

By the time Tina was clean, both Jody and Diane were laughing at her and at themselves. Stumbling and splashing to the bank, they deposited the little dog and then collapsed, watching her somersault and wiggle and roll and shake.

Only when the laughter subsided did Jody realize that Diane was crying. She had dropped her head to her knees. He couldn't see her face, only her shoulders lifting in spasms.

Tina, panting, hurled herself at him, demanding his lap. He shoved her aside. But he didn't know what to do for Diane, so he just sat there, waiting.

Finally she raised her head. Rubbing her swollen eyes, she said, almost crossly, "I can't waste time like this. I've got to find Moss."

"I'm really sorry," he told her. "I mean, it was great having you help. But I'm sorry about taking you away from looking."

She shook her head. "It was good to do something useful. Janet says we'll have to give up soon. See, she has the boys at home and a nursery that she and her husband run. She says if Moss turns up, the people here will call her. They'll be looking for him. He'll probably head for their barn or the trial field. He'll go where the sheep are. If he can."

"She must hate to leave without him."

Diane nodded. "He's a special dog. He belonged to her grandfather."

"I thought he belonged to your best friend."

"He does. But first he belonged to Janet's grandfather. It's a long story. And she's kept him this year, worked with him. Zanna's coming. That's my friend. She's coming for the summer, and if Moss is still gone, it'll be awful. See, it's my fault, because I sent him for the sheep. I thought I was some kind of hotshot. Boy, was I dumb!"

"You sent him?" Jody was brought up short. "I thought . . . you said only your friend knew how to work the dog."

Diane nodded. "But when she gets in a jam and can't figure which way to send him, she tells him to look back. Then he chooses the way to go after the sheep, wherever they are. So that's what I did. Maybe I was showing off. I don't know. Everyone was yelling. I was sure Moss could bring those sheep in from the back field. So I unhitched him and made him face that direction. And then I told him, 'Look back!' " She rose to her feet. "No one's seen him since. Janet says he may be holed up with sheep somewhere, sheep that got away. If he is, then probably he's all right. But he won't stand a chance against those coyotes."

"I bet he'll be all right," Jody told her. "He's so fast."

She sent him an unbelieving look. "Yeah, he's fast. Maybe he can outrun them. That is, if he can run at all." She looked up at a low dark cloud. "I better get going."

"Yeah. Me, too. They're probably all waiting."

"All?"

"Family," he said, remembering to be careful. "Good luck. I really mean it."

"Thanks," she said. "If you see Janet, tell her I'll head back in an hour or so."

Somewhere above them a hawk whistled shrilly. They both glanced up and then quickly down again as the cloud shifted and low sunlight drenched the riverbank in sudden, dazzling brilliance.

14

The car was gone, but not Mom. She was waiting for Jody in the parking area, and she was furious. Did he have any idea how long he'd been gone? Was he trying to blow their cover by forcing her to stand around like this?

He tried to explain, but she just pounced on his words and cut them off. He should have said where he was going. The river must be miles off.

Jody had had no idea. He only remembered the handler's telling him the river wasn't far. Now, after looking for it and letting Diane lead him there, he had a feeling he had walked miles. But that wasn't what made his mother so mad, so he didn't bother to go into it. He was tired. His feet were soaked and sore. He was starving.

She wouldn't let him get something to eat, though. He had to stay out of the way and keep an eye out for the car, which Marie had taken to drive Phil to his van. As soon as Marie got back here, they would take off for home.

"And stop for something on the way?" asked Jody.

"We had lunch," she said pointedly, "while we waited for you."

Jody didn't answer. He heard Janet's name called and then saw her unhitch Tess. His mother saw Janet, too, and said, "That's the woman whose dog's still missing. She doesn't even care enough to keep looking."

Jody's throat closed as if he had swallowed too much at a time. For a moment he couldn't breathe.

"What's the matter with you?" Mom sounded alarmed. "What's wrong?"

Jody shook his head. He gulped air. Then he managed to get out a few choked words: "You don't know. You don't know." Once the words, barely whispered, were released, his throat unclenched. He felt limp with relief.

"Are you sick?" she asked, touching his face. "You're all sweaty."

He shook his head. He didn't know what he was. He wished he had stayed with Diane. He wished he were home in his room. He wished he had never come here. He didn't want to leave without finding out what had happened to Moss. He didn't want to think about that dog anymore, not ever.

Aunt Marie drove down into the parking area. She moved out of the driver's seat without leaving the car and then jerked her head to direct Jody to the back on the far side so that he was unlikely to be seen getting in with his mother.

"So what happened?" she asked as they drove off. She asked Mom, not Jody.

"How did Tina get blood all over her?" Aunt Marie demanded after Mom gave a brief rundown.

Jody said, "I took her for a walk like you said. I didn't know there was blood on the ground. It was muddy, too."

"You should've told one of us. You should keep track of the time. You—"

"I've said that," Mom informed her. "He's not feeling too good. Leave him be."

Jody sank back. The little dog snuggled against him. He tried to push her off.

Up front his aunt was talking about future prospects when suddenly she cried out, "Look! What's that?"

Suddenly braked, the car swerved, slowed, and backed. Then it bumped along the shoulder. The little dog, hurled to the floor, tried to scramble back up. Jody ignored her. He had no idea where to look or what to look for.

When the car stopped, Mom and Aunt Marie got out at the same time and ran around behind it. Jody stayed inside, but he opened the window and craned to see what they were up to. At first there seemed to be nothing but the two women bent over what looked like a black trash bag.

Only when Mom straightened did he realize that the black thing was shaped like a dog. Dead? Dying maybe. He assumed it was a road casualty, the kind Mom sometimes managed to save if she could get it to her boss in time. But out here they were hours from home. What could she do for a dog that had been hit by a car on this lonely stretch of road?

Mom called Jody to bring her raincoat, which was stashed in back. "Hurry!" she shouted.

They always wanted him to hurry. But he ached after all that walking. He couldn't move quickly.

As he came up to them, his stomach took a tumble. This wasn't just any dog. It was a Border Collie. Him! Moss! Was it really Moss, or did Jody just wish it was?

"Is he going to be all right?" he asked, handing over the raincoat.

"No telling."

"We have to get him to a vet."

All the time they spoke, Mom and Aunt Marie were rolling the dog from side to side to get the raincoat under and then around him.

Jody tried to calculate the distance they had come. "How long will it take to get back to the trial?" he asked.

"We're not going back," Aunt Marie said as they lifted the wrapped dog and carried him to the car.

Mom said, "He has a better chance with us than with them. Open the door. Grab Tina."

"But they're looking for him," Jody protested as the little dog shot out of the car. He had to chase her down the embankment.

By the time he came back with Tina writhing in his grasp, Mom and Aunt Marie had the dog stretched out on the backseat.

"I'll take Tina up front," Marie told him. "You just watch the dog."

"Do you know where there's a vet around here?" Jody asked

as he slid in next to the dog's head. "They must know back at the trial. They already took one dog to a vet this morning."

"Jody," Mom said, "if we bring him back to those people, he's out of our hands. You understand? If they decide he's hopeless, if they give up on him, that'll be the end of him. At least with us he has a chance."

The dog stirred. Turning, Jody saw that one eye was swollen shut. Blood had already formed a crust around that side of his head. His ear was torn. Fresh blood seeped from an open wound that Jody couldn't see, but he heard it dripping on the raincoat.

Mom stopped at the first convenience store they came to. She told Jody to wait in the car while she and Aunt Marie went in. When they came back, they had paper towels and a plastic dish with water in it and some kind of baby medicine to give the dog energy. He actually lapped some water, but he didn't want the medicine. The dog began to shiver. Mom sopped up some of the blood. Aunt Marie took her jacket off and laid it over him. He closed his good eye.

Mom frowned. "Maybe we can tempt him with meat," she said. She went back into the store. When she came out, she had a sausage stick, which she unwrapped. It smelled spicy; it made Jody's mouth water. She broke off a small piece and held it close to the dog's muzzle. He actually licked it a bit, but when she placed it in his mouth, he let it fall on the seat. She tried again. This time he wouldn't touch it.

She ended up wetting a paper towel with the baby medicine and squeezing a trickle on to his tongue. When she stroked his throat to make him swallow, her hand came away all bloody. But she kept at it until he had taken almost a quarter of the bottle.

Nodding with satisfaction, she handed the sausage to Jody. "You can offer him some from time to time," she instructed.

"Did you find out about a vet?" he asked as they took to the road again.

"We asked," Marie said. "If he hadn't taken any nourishment, we might've had to stop around here. But of course he'd be recognized as a sheepdog. The vet would guess he was from the trial."

Jody waited for her to go on. When she didn't, he said. "So where will you take him? How long before he gets to a vet?"

"We'll see," Mom said. "He's had some electrolytes. The bleeding may slow. We'll just see."

"What about his owner?" Jody demanded.

"Plenty of time for the owner," Aunt Marie told him. "First we've got to save the dog."

Jody sighed. He supposed Mom knew what she was doing. Moss wouldn't be the first dog she had kept alive. Absently he raised the sausage to his mouth and chomped down on it. Then he realized he was stealing from the dog. He extracted the chewed sausage and set it on the dog's tongue. Moss shut his mouth, then opened it. The sausage was gone.

Jody wanted to shout out the news, but not here, not like this. He wanted Diane and Janet to know that Moss was alive and eating. Well, Mom would let them know before long. It was just a matter of time now, a few more hours of waiting and worrying.

He took another bite of sausage and swallowed it before he could stop himself. Never mind, there was more. The next piece would be for Moss.

15   Aunt Marie kept twisting around and asking Jody how the dog was doing. Like he was some expert on dogs? If she was so worried, why didn't she take him to a vet?

"He's resting," Jody finally told her. "Sleeping, maybe."

Mom pulled over to the side of the road and came around to the back. She opened the dog's good eye. She felt inside his mouth. "I thought you said he ate."

"He did."

"When?"

"Before. After we left the store."

"No, Brenda," Marie said from the front seat. "Don't stop. People around here must know about the sheepdog trial. They're bound to ask questions."

"Still . . ." Mom shook her head.

"Just keep going. Fast."

On they went, passing other cars, barely slowing as they came through towns.

It was at a four-way stop in one town that an officer motioned them to the side of the road right in front of a small police station.

"I'm sorry," Mom burst out as she handed over her license and registration. "I don't usually speed. But my dog's been hurt, and I need to get him to an animal hospital. I don't know any around here."

The officer looked in back. "What happened? A hit?"

Mom shook her head. "He was attacked."

The officer scowled. "Okay. Come into the station and we'll make a couple of calls. He looks like he needs attention right away."

Mom and the officer disappeared through the door of the station.

Jody said, "She lied to him."

Aunt Marie said, "She had to. If she says the dog isn't hers, they'll find out where he came from."

"They should," Jody insisted. "He belongs to Diane's friend. What if he dies and they never find out?"

"We're trying to keep him from dying, which is more than they'd do. Jody, if you don't get it, just shut up, will you? Don't mess with this."

Jody looked down at the dog, already messed beyond description. Was he dying? Jody touched the ear that wasn't torn. He was surprised to find it cold, really cold, even though a jacket covered the dog and the car was warm.

Mom and the police officer appeared. He got in a car and pulled ahead of Mom, who slid behind the wheel and took off. "He's got some vet to open up a hospital," she said. "It'll take us out of the way, but he thinks we'll be there in about ten minutes."

"Did he give you a ticket for speeding?" Jody asked her.

"Not yet. He told me I shouldn't endanger myself and others even when there's an emergency like this. I said I knew. I said I was sorry."

"Did you get your license back?" Aunt Marie asked her.

Mom shook her head. "He was concentrating on finding a vet. He's cool."

"Well, be careful. They'll want to know the dog's name."

"Moss," said Jody.

"No way," snapped his aunt. "We have to agree on a different name."

For some reason this bothered Jody more than he could say. He felt his stomach clench again.

"Lad?" said Mom.

"Lad's fine," Aunt Marie told her. "You hear that, Jody?"

His throat clogged. "I'm sick," he mumbled.

"We can't stop," Mom retorted. "That officer is leading us. I don't know the way."

"Open the window," Aunt Marie said. "You just need some fresh air."

Jody opened the window and stuck his face into the wind. Don't think about blood, he told himself. But when he turned back and saw the dog's hair blowing in blood-clotted spikes, he had to shut his eyes and lean his forehead against the window.

With his eyes closed he saw the sheep that had been killed, their legs waving above their torn, bloated bodies. He smelled them inside this car. Then he was sick on the floor where some of the dog's blood had already spilled.

"Use the paper towel," Mom told him. Then she spoke to Aunt Marie. "He felt funny before, too."

"Then he shouldn't've stuffed his face with sausage," Aunt Marie snapped back.

"He ate the sausage?" Mom said. "Jody, don't you have any sense at all?"

Jody kept his head down on his knees. Tears filled his eyes, and his nose ran. It was weird being like this. Anyone would think he was crying, which he wasn't.

After a while he blew his nose on a paper towel. Then he sort of mopped up his and Moss's mess. By the time the car slowed and pulled off the road and stopped in a driveway, Jody was able to hold his head up again.

The officer helped carry Moss inside before he drove away. Jody was left with Tina, who hopped from one seat to the other and panted at the closed windows. When Jody couldn't stand it any longer, he took the bunched paper towel in one hand, Tina's leash in the other, and walked across the small lawn to shrubbery where he could stuff the trash out of sight.

Mom and Aunt Marie were gone a long time. Clouds massed again, nearly shutting out the watery sun. Jody went back to the car and let Tina climb up beside him.

It rained once more, not heavily, but just enough to shroud the car in wet gloom. When Moss was carried onto the backseat, raindrops glistened on what remained of his coat. Half of his head was shaved, stitches like angry scratches crisscrossing over and around his ear and neck and throat. There were more stitches along his bare shoulder and down behind one foreleg. His tongue lolled from his slack mouth. Except that he was snoring, he looked dead.

Mom paused after she tucked the jacket around him. "Maybe we should've let the vet keep him overnight like he said."

"No," Aunt Marie told her. "You'd have to come all the way back here. We've got to clear out for good. Anyway, he's had antibiotics. What more will he need?"

"I don't know. If he goes into shock again . . ." Mom's words trailed off.

"He's had stuff for shock. Let's just get him home, where you can look after him."

Mom sounded anxious, though. "We may need gas," she said as she started up the car. "What's left for money?"

Aunt Marie opened up her bag and dug inside. "Six dollars is all. This rescue cost us a bundle."

"We bit off more than we can chew," Mom answered with

another backward glance at the dog stretched out on the back-seat. She hunched forward, driving slowly now, as if she weren't exactly sure where she was heading.

16

Minutes after Jody got home from school, Mom called from work and told him to take the dogs out to the yard separately and to keep Tina away from the Border Collie. Jody noticed that she didn't say the dog's name, not Moss, not Lad. Maybe she didn't want to start an argument. Or maybe she was just too tired after being up all night tending the injured dog.

To take Tina out the back door, Jody had to pass through the kitchen, where Moss was lying. He had moved from the dog bed to the bare floor, where he lay on his good side. He didn't even look up at Jody and Tina. Skittering over to Moss, she greeted him with quick dabs of her tongue. The bigger dog merely turned his head aside as if she were a buzzing fly he was trying to avoid. Jody clipped the leash to her collar and dragged her through the door for her five-minute outing.

After she was put away in the living room with the cats, he approached Moss with the leash. But there was nothing to attach it to. Of course Moss's collar had been removed. Most of his neck and throat had been shaved and stitched.

Jody puzzled over this predicament. He owed it to Diane and her friend to keep Moss safe until they had him back, but he guessed Moss was in no condition to run away from him. So he opened the door to the yard and spoke to the dog. "Moss! Come!"

Moss actually raised his head and then half rose before flopping down again. Jody went over and bent down to him. "Come on, boy," he said, "let's go." Again the dog drew himself partway up. When Jody reached around to lift him to his feet, the dog winced, his muscles tightening at Jody's touch. Dropping to his knees, Jody moved his hands away from the injured foreleg and eased Moss up.

That's how they progressed to the door, Moss unsteady on three legs and Jody crawling beside him with one hand underneath for support. Moss wouldn't attempt the back steps, and he looked too heavy for one person to carry. What if Jody tried and then dropped him? Probably Aunt Marie and Mom had taken him out together before they went to work this morning.

Jody looked around. If only there was someone nearby to help. He let himself out the yard gate and ran next door. The neighbor's back bell didn't seem to work, so he knocked. When no one came, he started around the house. But the car wasn't parked out front. No one was home.

He ran back to find that Moss had gotten himself down the steps anyway. The dog was wobbling across the lawn toward the side fence, where he teetered as he tried to lift a hind leg. Jody wanted to help him, but Moss just stopped when Jody took hold of him. So Moss ended up squatting like a puppy to pee. When he was finished, he crept under a bush and eased himself down in its shade.

It was exactly how he had picked his own spot under Janet's van. It seemed important to Jody that he recall everything he could about Moss, especially a few of the exact words sheepdogs were trained to obey. Then he would be able to handle this dog without hurting him. He'd better be careful, though, more careful than Diane had been when she sent Moss into unknown danger. You didn't say, "Look back!" to a dog like this unless you wanted him to run far and wide in search of sheep. What were some of the other commands? The only one Jody was absolutely sure of was "That'll do." He had heard handlers speaking that phrase again and again, not only to tell a dog its run was finished but also to call a dog to attention.

He took a few steps away from the dog and spoke his name. Moss just eyed him from beneath the bush. Then Jody said with more conviction than he felt, "Moss, that'll do! Come!"

The words reached somewhere inside the dog. He heaved himself sideways and then up onto three legs.

"Good boy," Jody told him. "Here, come." The dog hobbled after him, then faltered at the porch steps. This time, instead of grabbing the dog, Jody used his chest like a sling to keep the dog from sliding backward as he boosted the hindquarters one step at a time. It was slow going. By the time they made it up to the door and into the kitchen, Moss was panting as if he had run a course. He staggered to the water bowl Jody's mother had left out for him and then slid down in front of it to drink.

Watching him splash much of the water onto the floor, Jody figured that even drinking must be painful for the dog. Maybe the stitches were too tight. Maybe there was something wrong inside his mouth that the vet had missed yesterday. When would Mom take Moss to Dr. Weddell, the vet she worked for?

Gently he shoved Moss out of the wetness and sort of mopped up the spill. There was nothing more to be done. Yet he didn't want to walk away from this dog, which had been lying alone, and hurting, in a strange place all day.

When Mom walked into the kitchen, she found Jody sitting on the floor, his back against the stove. Moss lay on his side, his head just inches from Jody's hand. They weren't touching. They were just together.

She flew to the dog. "What happened? What's wrong?"

Jody roused himself. "Nothing. He's been out."

"So what are you doing?" she demanded.

He didn't know how to answer. Of course the last thing she expected was to find him on the floor like this. Never before had he taken the slightest interest in any of her rescued animals.

He looked down at Moss and then up at his mother. "I don't know," he finally mumbled. "Just hanging out, I guess."

17 Through the week, even after Aunt Marie's boyfriend had built a ramp for the back porch, Moss was never let out alone. Mom was afraid he would find a way through or under the fence. A farm dog couldn't deal with all the cars in their neighborhood, and there was heavy truck traffic just two streets away. Besides, a dog on three legs was not only slow but clumsy.

"If his appetite picked up," she said, "he'd heal faster."

"Right," Aunt Marie said. "It's like he's depressed."

Supper over, they watched Moss lick once or twice at the frying pan full of leftovers. Then he turned away listlessly.

"Maybe he's homesick," Jody suggested.

Mom said, "Homesick for a three-foot chain?"

Aunt Marie said, "Forget it, Jody. He's not going back until we're sure he's worth keeping. We've already seen what they do to the dogs that can't work."

"When will we be sure?" he asked.

Mom said, "The vet I'm taking him to on Saturday may have an idea of how much he can recover."

Aunt Marie said, "You're not taking him to Dr. Weddell, are you?"

Mom shook her head. "No, I'm going to take Laddie to someone way out of town. I'll tell her what we said to the vet up-country and also that we just moved here. She won't suspect anything."

Jody pushed back his chair.

"Stomach bothering you again?" Mom asked.

He shook his head. Maybe it was, just a little. Or maybe the things he wanted to say but couldn't ended up in an undigestible lump in his stomach.

He had to wade through the cats. Most of them clamored at the kitchen door because they, along with Tina, were still kept out of Moss's space. Two of them had consoled themselves for being barred from the kitchen by staking out a claim to Jody's bed. He managed to eject them and shut his door. He needed to figure out a way to let Moss's family know that their dog was alive without telling on Mom and Aunt Marie.

Once or twice over the past few days he had suspected that Mom might be having doubts about keeping Moss like this. Probably his unresponsiveness undermined her confidence. Still, on the surface everything seemed normal. She and Aunt Marie were already plotting some new mission. That was the problem. When Mom got together with Aunt Marie and Phil, they made her feel good. It was sort of like brainwashing.

Jody decided he would have to bide his time. On Saturday he asked if he could go along for Moss's vet appointment. That put his mother on guard.

"To make trouble?" she demanded. "You have something up your sleeve?"

He shook his head. "I just want to hear what the vet says."

"I'll tell you," she said.

He could feel his own bulk standing in her way. "I took care of him all week," he pleaded, "every single day after school."

She nodded. "All right. But keep your mouth shut about, you know, things."

Together they carried Moss to the car, not because he couldn't get there on his own three feet, but because it meant he didn't have to wear a collar.

The vet took her time examining him.

"You're such a good boy, Laddie," Mom crooned to him.

Jody thought she might give herself away. It was so obvious that Moss wasn't listening. Could the vet detect this? Did she notice that the dog didn't care?

"Your dog?" The vet was speaking to Jody.

He glanced at his mother before nodding.

"A family dog," Mom quickly said. "But Jody and Lad have a special relationship. He takes him out every day after school."

"Well"—the vet continued, still addressing Jody—"you've kept him very fit. If he hadn't been in such good condition, he'd be a lot worse off. Now," she added, "it's time to start some aggressive therapy. Walking first, and then—"

"Walking while he's still on three legs?" Mom asked.

"Absolutely. It will encourage him to put some weight on the injured one."

"You think he will?" Jody asked her.

The vet said, "It's hard to predict. There's been some nerve damage, no question about that. You don't want the surrounding muscle to atrophy. You understand? If he's inactive, then maybe he loses the chance to come back. If he's exercised, the leg itself may find a way to compensate. Even if he's left with a limp, he can still play and thrive. That's what you aim for."

"Will he—" Jody broke off. His mother was staring hard at him. She must have guessed that he was going to ask about working, not playing.

The vet smiled. "Let's take this a little bit at a time. So far so good. The vet who sewed him up did a fine job, but I can't remove all the stitches today. And the antibiotics ought to continue until the ear dries up. It doesn't look like he's been scratching it, but he may get restless as he feels better." She turned to Jody's mother. "Border Collies are high-energy dogs. I guess you must know that. How long have you had him?"

Mom spoke almost too quickly. "Three years or so."

"Good." The vet nodded approvingly. "Then you've had him all his life. If you survived his puppy months, you'll understand that he needs exercise. Your son can start with short walks. Lad will let you know when he's ready for more."

"You mean longer walks?" Jody asked.

"That, and running. But wait for more healing before you start jogging with him. And no ball games for a while, no Frisbee. Nothing with sharp turns. You'll see. He'll show you when he's ready."

"Do you wish you worked for her?" Jody asked when they got Moss into the car.

Mom laughed. "She's nice, all right, but she may be too sharp for comfort. She nearly got me with that question about how long we'd had the dog."

"How did you guess his age?" Jody asked, thinking that the vet hadn't been trying to trip Mom up. Mom and Aunt Marie had this hang-up about secrecy. They seemed to think that every-one was snooping, trying to catch them breaking the law.

"I was lucky," Mom said. "The vet we saw last Sunday guessed Lad was three or four." Then she added, "You okay about walking him? People will ask questions. We're going to have to agree on a story. You hear? And I don't want you pushing him. I don't care how nice this vet is. She didn't see him when he was really bad."

Jody nodded. What did Mom think he was going to do out front where people would see him? He knew what he looked like when he wasn't even huffing and puffing from exertion. He wasn't about to start jogging in public.

"We'll have to rig up a collar that won't dig into his neck," she said a moment later. "I'll figure out something."

Before she went out with Aunt Marie and Phil, she ripped up a scarf, braided it, and knotted it loosely around Moss's neck. "There," she crooned, stroking the dog on the good side of his head. "Now you're in business."

Moss suffered her attention without meeting her eyes or shifting his body in the slightest acknowledgment of her touch.

She paused in the doorway. "What do you think it'll take to get this dog to wag his tail?" she wondered out loud.

"Years, maybe," Aunt Marie responded. "Those sheepdogs are so ground down they don't know what kindness is."

Jody kept silent. Maybe he was beginning to learn a thing or two about concealment himself.

  As soon as Moss was given the run of the house, he found the front door and set himself down in front of it.

Jody's mother showed him the back door into the fenced yard. "You want to go out?" she asked him.

Moss merely returned to his front door vigil, his entire being striving to reach the other side and beyond. Even Tina bouncing all around him left him unmoved.

"He wants to go home," Jody said.

"Well, he can't," Mom told him. "At least not yet."

She worried about his slipping away. She made signs for the door warning people to be careful whenever they opened it. She tried to distract him with games of fetch or hide-and-seek. Moss didn't fetch. He didn't hide. And the only seeking he did was no game.

It was like a contest, Mom ever more inventive and indulgent, the dog steadfast and resistant.

"It's up to you," Mom finally told Jody. "Maybe walking him somewhere new will perk him up."

Jody, who had avoided all the places where he might run into kids from school, began to venture away from his own neighborhood. He walked with his shoulders slightly hunched, his eyes downcast. He had no trouble with Moss, who seldom strayed from his side to sniff or pee along the way. With his head and tail held low, he seemed to mimic Jody's stance, the leash connecting them almost always slack.

Jody didn't tell anyone what he was learning from this dog, that "stay" prevented Moss from trying to nudge past him at the door, and "get behind" kept Moss from pulling ahead. The more time they spent together, the more Moss taught him. And it wasn't all to do with commands. Things along the way were like signals to the dog. The fence around the playground they passed almost every day always brought Moss up short. For an instant he would halt, raise his head, and scan the area beyond. It didn't take much to understand that the wire fence sparked a glimmer of hope in him. His ears would flatten as he turned from the playing children and their caretakers. Not his kind of livestock behind this fence, not his business.

Then one day someone did turn up in the playground, only not for Moss.

"Hey, Jody!" Tara Trevino walked toward him, two small kids in tow. "What happened to your dog?"

"He's not mine," Jody said. "My mother's keeping him for someone who can't take care of him." This was the explanation they had rehearsed.

"Well, whatever," said Tara. "What happened to him?"

Jody told her Moss had been attacked by coyotes.

"No kidding. Coyotes? That's pretty serious. Where?"

"Up-country," he replied. "My mother works for a vet." He broke off. He had a feeling he was about to say too much. Tara, who had been in his homeroom all last year, had never even spoken to him before.

One of the children stuck her fingers through the fence. Tara pulled her arm back. "How is he with kids?" she asked.

"I don't know." Then Jody remembered Diane's mentioning that her friend who owned Moss was coming for the summer to help out with Janet's boys. "They've got kids where he comes from." Jody added, "so he must be used to them."

"Wait a minute," Tara said, "we'll come out." She turned to the child whose arm she still held. "Want to go see the doggy?" When the child nodded, she picked up the smaller one, stuffed her into a stroller, and set off toward the gate.

Jody walked Moss along the fence line to meet Tara as she and the kids emerged from the playground.

"Don't let them touch the sore spots," he warned. He spoke softly to Moss, echoing the tone he had heard Janet and Diane use. When he told him to lie down, Moss lowered himself stiffly, protecting his injured foreleg from pressing against the asphalt.

Tara approached first. She touched Moss's head and back. Jody was astonished to see a slow, slight waving of tail. He tucked this away along with the language he was learning with Moss. Now Jody had an inkling that Moss could respond to someone who reminded him of Diane. Who reminded him, no doubt, of his owner, Diane's best friend. This knowledge might come in handy later on.

Not that Tara, who was built like a basketball player, looked anything like Diane. But it wasn't hard to figure that whatever Moss saw in each girl had little to do with appearance.

The child who had wanted to reach through the fence now tried to encircle Moss's neck in a hug. Jody and Tara intervened at the same time. The child, thwarted again, burst out crying. Tara explained about the sore spots on the dog's neck. Jody glanced around, terrified that someone would come over to find out what the trouble was and start asking questions about the dog.

Tara took the child's hand and placed it on the dog's shoulder. "Pat him there where his fur is," she said. "Right there."

Sniffling, the child patted Moss, who turned to lick her tear-stained face. She chortled as he cleaned her up. The younger child strained from the stroller.

Lifting her out, Tara said, "This beats the playground. Do you walk him every day?"

Jody nodded. "Your sisters seem crazy about dogs," he said. "Do you have one at home?"

Tara told him they weren't her sisters. They were her neighbor's kids, and she got paid to baby-sit for three hours every weekday afternoon. "I can't even do homework, because I'm supposed to watch them every single, solitary minute. You know how boring it gets sitting in a playground with a bunch of screaming kids?" She eyed him. "You get bored with the dog?"

"Sometimes." He lied because he figured it was cool to be bored.

"Maybe we should team up," she said. "I'm not allowed to walk in the park without someone else along. For safety. We could explore if we went together."

Jody nodded. What was he getting himself into? There was no time to consider whether the good of it outweighed the bad. He didn't even know what the bad might be. All he could be sure of was that Moss liked Tara and had comforted the kid.

"What's his name?" the child asked.

Jody only hesitated a second before telling the truth. It couldn't make any difference to his mother and aunt if this kid and someone he barely knew called the dog by his proper name. Besides, think how much it might mean to Moss, who had actually shown a flicker of interest in Tara.

They agreed to get together the next day after school if it didn't rain. Since Tara needed time to give the kids a snack first, he would meet her more than halfway to the park. It was farther than he had taken Moss up to now. He told himself that if it turned out to be too much for the dog, they wouldn't make a practice of it.

But he walked home almost lighthearted and with his head up for a change. If after nearly two weeks Moss was turning a corner in his recovery, he might be ready to go home a lot sooner than Mom or Aunt Marie expected.

19 As Moss grew stronger, so did his resistance to Jody's mother and aunt and their friends. When the vet saw him again, she was clearly impressed with his recovery. But at home he remained listless and unresponsive. Something had to be done.

When CAATS got together again, Jody thought they were in his house to plan some new major rescue that required organization. But when he heard Lad's name crop up, he opened his door to listen.

The conversation in the living room had already progressed to a proposal that Lad might need to be an only dog. If Brenda could place Tina in a good home, that might make a difference to the Border Collie. It was worth trying.

Someone offered to take Tina for a week or so, but Mom said she had already made overtures to a very nice couple whose little dog had died. They were waiting to get past the worst of their bereavement before taking Tina on trial. Actually Mom said, there had been one or two other good prospects coming through reception at the animal hospital. But this couple seemed like such a perfect match that she had decided to give them a little more time.

"Call them," Phil advised. "Tell them you have to make room for another dog."

Aunt Marie said, "We sort of thought of adopting her ourselves. She's such a cheerful little thing. She never mopes like Lad."

Phil said, "You can't keep a dog that belonged to someone who works near where you work."

Aunt Marie sighed. "I know. I just wish it was Lad we had to unload first. With his attitude, it'll be a job and a half finding a home for him."

Why was she talking about finding Moss a home? He was going back to Janet as soon as he was well enough. Listening for Mom to set Marie straight, Jody heard his own name spoken. Then Phil said, "Brenda's right. Talk about attitude changing. Lad's probably the first animal Jody's taken any interest in."

"And once school's out," Mom added, "he'll be dying for something to do."

Flinging the door wide, Jody stormed into the living room. "By summer Moss should be home where he belongs," he blurted.

Silence greeted this announcement.

"If you're eavesdropping," Aunt Marie told him, "you might as well come in here."

Jody hadn't meant to confront them like this. It was between him and Mom. But he had no choice now. So he said, "Moss— Lad doesn't need to be placed somewhere." He faced his mother. "You said when he's ready. You said—"

She stopped him. "Yes, Jody. But we don't yet know whether he can ever be a useful dog again the way he was. You understand?"

He nodded. He wouldn't announce to all of them that he was going to see to it that Moss was fit for work. "It's what he lives for," he mumbled. "You saw him before."

"How do you know he lives for that?" Aunt Marie broke in. "Maybe it was all he ever had."

Arguments welled up. Jody didn't know how to deliver them.

Mom said, "Listen Jody, if Lad's never able to run faster than sheep, he'll be no good on a farm. We have to wait and see. In the meantime we're trying to lift his spirits, to get him interested in being alive. Doesn't that make sense? Right now he's like someone disabled that can't come to terms with how his life has changed. You can help. You already help by walking him like you do. And if you show him how to play, that could turn him around. That can be your job now, your goal, while we try out other . . . possibilities. Okay?"

"Okay," he said, because when she put it like that, it did make sense. But he went back to his room thinking he'd better not give himself away again.

He wished he could talk to someone. Not Tara. Even though they had taken a few walks together, they weren't likely to get on closer terms. That was clear after the first time he passed her in the hall at school and she steered away from him.

Later, when she tried to explain to Jody why she had snubbed him, he had shrugged her off. He didn't need to hear that she couldn't afford to be seen with a dork like him. Maybe she was too close to being one herself. Just last fall she was still running around the street with a hockey stick, and even Jody knew that was uncool. Now she had those two little kids to drag around. If he helped trim the edge off her boredom and she showed him places he'd never been to before, that was a fair enough trade. There was no reason to expect more from her.

But he couldn't help wondering what Diane and Janet must be going through now that almost three weeks had passed since the dog had vanished. He couldn't help wishing that he were able to trust one person enough to lay out everything about Moss. One person who would understand and maybe even think of a way to help him out of this predicament.

20 After Tina left the household, Mom and Aunt Marie looked for a difference in Moss's attitude. But he still refused to grant them more than a passing notice. As far as they could tell, he did nothing all day but stare at the front door.

Jody did detect a change, although he wasn't sure that it had anything to do with Tina's departure. Maybe it just reflected Moss's improved condition now that he was getting out for longer walks.

Since Tara had introduced Jody to the park, he had begun to explore the wooded paths that were too rough for the stroller. Usually Tara turned back before the little kids got too tired and cranky. But after Jody walked them out to the street, he didn't always go home. He had found that if he climbed over the steep hill and descended to the stream, it led to railroad tracks that formed a long, empty road. In spite of trash that littered the bank, the remoteness of the place made him think of the river where he and Diane had bathed Tina. It was the closest he had ever been to wilderness. Not that he remembered much; that day most of his attention had been diverted by Diane's misery.

Now he had plenty of time. Even though it was good to have Tara's company on many of his outings, he was beginning to get used to walks alone with Moss. Squirrels and chipmunks would scramble out of his path and then freeze like plastic ornaments. Once in a while Moss paused to eye them, his ears erect. Usually they responded to his stare by chittering fiercely. Then he would duck his head and leave them to their frantic dartings.

Sometimes when they met walkers with dogs running free, Moss would pull on the leash. To make up for holding him prisoner, Jody started jogging along the tracks, each day going a little farther, slowing or turning back only when they both were out of breath.

So it didn't surprise him when he arrived home from school one day to discover that Moss had abandoned his vigil at the door. He had a new occupation, keeping the cats in line. All nine of them were huddled together at one end of the sofa. Jody halted a moment to see what Moss was up to. But aside from one swift glance in Jody's direction, the dog would not loosen his grip on the situation.

There was no telling when he had herded them together or how long he had kept them there. But the cats seemed resigned. When one of them made the slightest adjustment in its position, Moss instantly flanked that way until the errant cat had melted back into the furry cluster.

Beyond that, Moss didn't seem to have an extended game plan. His job was to gather and hold. Now it was up to someone else. To Jody.

"That'll do," Jody told him.

Moss backed off. Released, two of the cats hopped down to the floor. In a flash Moss turned them back to the couch.

"That'll do," Jody repeated.

Moss flung him a look that seemed to challenge the command. Couldn't Jody see that the cats would escape and all of Moss's work would be undone?

"I know," Jody said. "That'll do, Moss." He reached for the leash hanging on the doorknob. The only way to distract Moss was to get him out of the house.

That day Jody walked Moss all the way to a warehouse loading dock that backed up to the tracks. For a while they stood and watched a man with a forklift stacking pallets. Moss was attentive here. Did the forklift sound like a farm tractor?

When the man finally shut off the engine and jumped to the ground, Moss leaned toward him. Once again Jody saw that slow, slight wave of the tail that almost combined a question with a greeting. The man nodded at Jody. Then he stopped. "That a sheepdog?" he asked. "Looks like he got himself tangled up good. Barbed wire or what?"

Jody gave the rehearsed answer, adding, "Most people don't know what he is."

The man walked over to Moss and held out his hand. Moss let him cup his muzzle. "Smartest dogs in the world. You ever seen them work?"

Jody was dying to boast about Moss, but all he said was that he had.

"Up to the Chiswick Fair. You never saw anything like it. I try to go every year. It's where I'm from. You ever been?"

Jody shook his head.

"You should get to it. I always visit home around then, second weekend in August. You wouldn't believe what them dogs can do."

Moss stood quietly, his head resting on the man's hands.

"Do you know any of the people?" Jody asked. "The sheepdog handlers?"

The man shook his head. "But I recognize some. They come year after year." He looked down at Moss. "It's a waste really. They need something to do, these dogs."

"I know," Jody said. "But some of them can't. If they're like hurt—or too old."

"You know what I like about the old dogs?" the man went on. "I like how slow and easy they can move them sheep around, like they've all the time in the world. I've seen some of those old fellas show the young fast ones a thing or two." He flashed a gap-toothed grin at Jody. "Maybe I take a shine to the old ones because I've got some age on me, too. I suppose I'm prejudiced."

Jody said, "I don't know where that fair is you're talking about. Maybe my dad will take me."

"Chiswick," the man told him. "It's got trotting horses and pig scrambles and rides and freaks like two-headed calves. But I always head for the dog trial. That's where you'll find me."

Jody had to tug Moss to get him away from the man. "Maybe I'll see you there," he said as he turned away.

"Bring the dog," the man called back as he headed for the warehouse. "He'll get a charge out of it."

Jody and Moss jogged a long way before they slowed to a walk. By the time they reached home, Mom was already there, the cats were fed, and the phone was ringing.

Jody flopped down in front of the television to watch an old *Star Trek* rerun.

---

21 Mom and Aunt Marie had another mall rescue. They wanted Jody's help, but it was planned for the Saturday he was supposed to go to his father's.

Jody figured it would sort itself out. As far as he was concerned, it was a toss-up. Having to stand watch at the mall like some total geek was about his least favorite thing. But then spending the day with his father could be pretty tough, too.

Still, it was a new twist to hear his parents argue over him.

"School's out in another week," said Mom at the door. "You can have him any day then."

"Like I don't work for a living?" Dad replied.

"We already have plans." she argued. Jody thought she made

it sound like a picnic or something. "His regular day was last weekend. When you canceled, I figured you wouldn't see him till next month."

"I just had to postpone. Sharon's folks were here. I told you."

"You never give a thought to other people's schedules," Mom retorted.

Dad looked past her at Jody. "You busy today or something?"

Jody shrugged. "I was going to meet a friend," he said, meaning Tara. "Me and her hang out sometimes when I walk the dog."

Dad's eyebrows shot up. "A girlfriend?"

"Not exactly," Jody mumbled. He was aware of his mother's stare. "Just someone from school," he added, feeling boxed in. When would he learn to keep his mouth shut?

"You've never mentioned any girl before." His mother sounded almost accusing. "I thought you went out on account of Lad."

"I do. We go lots of places without her, too. But she has to, like, baby-sit this afternoon. We take the kids and the dog to the park."

Both parents seemed to be processing this information.

Dad was the first to speak up. "Why don't you bring the dog, then, and come with me? I can drop you off after lunch."

Jody was quick to accept this offer. If he had Moss with him and Dad knew he was going to be outdoors later on, he would probably escape the usual routine of baseball practice.

Mom objected. She said she hadn't spent all this time and money on the dog to risk losing him or setting him back in his recovery.

Dad cast his eyes over Moss. "Doesn't look that bad," he

declared. "Nothing's going to happen to him. And," he added on a challenging note, "you can see they're buddies, Jody and the dog. I would've thought you'd encourage that."

Mom faltered. It was clear to Jody that she didn't want Moss out of her own sphere. Didn't she realize that he and the dog had been all over the neighborhood? Lots of people must have noticed Moss because of the wounds. Even now with the hair beginning to fuzz in over the bare skin, he must catch people's attention.

So he said, "It's not like Tina, where someone might recognize her. People around here don't even know what kind of dog he is."

"Get his leash," Dad told Jody.

After they pulled away from the curb, Dad said, "So this is the dog Thelma and Louise found on the side of the road? What was it she said? 'Like trash'?"

"Not really," Jody told him. "I mean, it's not like he was thrown away or anything."

"No?" Dad glanced over at the dog sitting on Jody's feet. "You were there?"

Jody nodded. "Moss was at the sheepdog trial. I saw him work. I talked to a kid that's the best friend of the person he belongs to."

Dad scowled, although whether at this information or at the car he was passing, Jody couldn't tell. After a moment Dad asked, "Does the kid know you've got him?"

"No," said Jody. "It would blow everyone's cover. They could be arrested for stealing, even though they're not. They're just keeping him till they're sure he's well enough to go home."

Dad threw him a look. "You buy that?"

At first Jody didn't answer. Then his voice dropped as he spoke: "I think he's almost ready now. To work. I know he wants to. See, I run with him every day. We go miles."

Dad shot him another glance. "Running?"

"Yes, to build him up. The vet said I could. But I can't let him off the leash because Mom says he'll be killed or stolen."

"Stolen! That's a laugh and a half. He's stolen already."

"No," Jody protested. "She promised he'd go home when he's strong enough. Otherwise they might shoot him. But I don't think they would."

"They?"

"Janet, the person he lives with. I just don't think she'd shoot him like they did the other dog that got torn up. Mom says they should've taken the dog to a vet to try to save him. That's what she did with Moss, and she's taken care of him the whole time. So she wants to be sure, that's all."

Dad glanced down at the dog again. "Maybe she'll let you keep him," he said.

Jody shook his head. "He's not mine. He's sad. He hates our house."

"How do you know?" Dad asked him.

Jody shrugged. "He's like depressed."

Dad grunted.

Jody was tempted to tell about the cat herding. He thought it would make his father laugh. This was the longest conversation they had had in ages. But the dog pressing on his feet reminded him to hold back, to be like Moss, who never gave himself away, at least not to the people who held him captive.

Jody never could guess in advance whom Moss might take to. So far there were only Tara and the forklift driver. Even then Moss didn't drop his reserve altogether. It was simply that he wasn't entirely aloof with them, as if he half expected them to be someone he was waiting for. Jody was beginning to think that Moss had an inner strength that you only read about in books or see in movies.

So Jody was completely unprepared to see Moss walk straight up to Sharon with his head raised and the tip of his tail swinging like a pendulum winding down.

"You're a sorry sight," Sharon said to the dog. He turned slightly and leaned his shoulder against her. She spoke to Jody. "You sure he's housebroken?"

Jody told her that Moss stayed in all day until he took him out after school.

"A dog's life." murmured Sharon. "He must be bored to death."

"He has the cats," Jody said. "Then when I get home, we have a long walk. And now that he's better, we run, too."

"Picture that," his father remarked. "Let's drive out to the reservoir and give him a real run for his money."

"Cool!" The reservoir was way out of town. They had gone fishing there a few summers ago before the cops started to enforce the city ordinance against using the public water supply for recreation.

"You want to eat first?" Sharon asked.

Jody shook his head. If they didn't get going, Dad might change his mind.

Jody noticed a brief glance, almost like surprise, pass between Sharon and his father. He guessed it had something to do with the unexpected presence of the dog until it occurred to him that they might just be taking note of his new priority. Not food first, not now, but Moss.

22 It was crowded with three people and a dog in the cab. Jody tried to shrink against the door to make room for Sharon, who took up even more space than he did. Noticing, she asked him if it was her fragrance that bothered him. Then she laughed and swiveled toward Dad and began talking to him about something else. Jody relaxed enough to savor the prospect of showing Moss a new place.

Dad parked off the road near a gap in the fence that led to the path that encircled the reservoir. They weren't the only people there, and Moss wasn't the only dog. At first they just walked along at a leisurely pace. Then, as the path curved away from the road, Dad started to jog.

Jody let him get far enough ahead so that there was no chance of his seeing Jody lurching after him. Then he took off with Moss at his side. As the distance between Jody and his father increased, Jody glanced back at Sharon, who was still walking. She waved him on. Now he was still farther behind Dad. He figured he could use Moss as an excuse for not catching up. Anything to avoid having to come under Dad's scornful eye.

Moss kept darting glances at the geese and ducks in the water. After a while he crossed the path in front of Jody to get to the water side. Jody stumbled and managed to keep from falling to his knees. But up ahead his father was checking back and probably caught a glimpse of Jody nearly tripping over the leash.

"Let him go," Dad shouted.

"Not allowed to," Jody called back.

"Bull!" his father declared. "Give the dog a break."

Jody looked all around. The fence would keep Moss from dashing directly onto the road. But he could pass Dad in one direction or Sharon in the other.

"Come on," Dad yelled. "Just let go."

Jody dropped the leash.

Dad called, "Here, boy. Here, Moss!" The call fell on deaf ears. Moss just stood beside Jody and gazed at the waterfowl.

So Dad resumed running, and after a moment Jody did, too. There was only a slight delay before Moss trotted along as well. At first he stayed as close as before. Then gradually he began to drift down the steep bank. He kept up with Jody, but now they were farther apart. Even though Jody realized that he could grab the leash if he needed to, he couldn't help feeling uneasy. If anything went wrong, it would be his fault.

On they went, Dad pulling farther ahead, Sharon falling farther behind, and Moss weaving around trees and rocks. When his leash snagged on a root, he sent Jody an expectant look. Jody clambered down the incline to free up the leash. Experimentally Jody told Moss to stay. The dog stood. Jody made him wait there until he had returned to the path. Relief and confidence surged up in him. Savoring this sense of command, he held back an extra moment before saying, "That'll do."

No sooner were the words spoken than Moss was plunging downward. He stopped for an instant, as if awaiting confirmation of his release, and then leaped out over the water. Landing with a splash, he vanished beneath the surface and then reappeared some distance from shore among a flock of startled geese.

Jody watched openmouthed, unable to recall any phrase that Moss might recognize and respond to. Most of the geese flapped up from the water and without actually flying removed themselves from the dog's orbit. But two parent geese with half-grown goslings stretched their necks out at him and hissed menacingly. Then one tried to lead the youngsters toward the main flock while the other parent kept up its attack on Moss.

No longer trusting "That'll do," Jody tried to tell Moss, "No!" But it didn't even get his attention. Either it wasn't a sheepdog word, or else Moss had water in his ears.

The goose protecting its brood looked dangerous. What if it pecked Moss in the eye? What if it grabbed his tail and pulled him under?

In a panic Jody cried, "No!" again. Then out of nowhere a real command came to him. Without thinking, he shouted, "Moss, look back!" Only then did delayed recognition hit him. This was what Diane had said to Moss when she could think of nothing else. That was what had sent Moss on his last gather of sheep already scattered and lost in the dark.

The command made Moss leave the aggressive goose and paddle after the main flock. Not only were they out in deeper water, but he set off as if in a true outrun, swimming wide in order to come behind them. When he tired, he would be far from shore. Jody expected him to disappear beneath the surface at any moment.

As Moss closed in on the flock, some of the geese took to the air. Jody could hear them winging overhead.

He wasn't aware that his father had doubled back until he spoke. "You want to try calling him? At least he knows you."

Jody drew a breath that was partly a sob. He shook his head.

"Why not?"

"I sent him," Jody answered. "It was all I could think of to get him away from the one that was attacking him."

"So tell him to quit."

Jody was afraid to try. He pictured what he had seen at the sheepdog trial, how one dog after another completed the task and then was called off with a "That'll do." If Moss managed to gather the geese and bring them toward shore, that would be the time when he might take the command and return. But could Moss keep paddling long enough to fetch the remaining geese?

"What are you waiting for?" Dad demanded.

Jody shook his head. The geese were turned now. If they came straight toward Jody, the longest part of Moss's swim was over. A few flapped off to one side. Moss flanked out to regroup them. Others submerged and broke away. It seemed to Jody that the dog was slowing down. "Good boy," he called, "good Moss."

"Good boy, nothing," said Jody's father. "Get that dog the hell out of the water."

More geese had to be hemmed in. Moss was making progress. Had he completed enough of the task to accept its finish and quit?

Thinking only of how Moss would react, Jody scrambled down to the water's edge and waded out toward the approaching flock. "Good boy," he said once more, and then: "That'll do, Moss, here."

Moss veered off, and the flock instantly dispersed into smaller groups that seemed to float off from the shore. Moss paddled toward Jody, who lost his footing just as they made contact.

It was a clumsy reunion, the dog thrashing the water as Jody clutched at him and pulled him down. Moss, desperate to stay above the surface, raked Jody's arms. When they staggered out together, Moss just stood, his sides heaving, unwilling or unable to climb the bank. Jody sank down and pulled off his water-logged sneakers.

By now Sharon had reached them. "What was that all about?" she asked.

Moss shook and then lay down to lick his paws and belly. Jody leaned over until his forehead grazed the mended ear with its new growth of fine hair, now soaked and parted to reveal the jagged line that had been stitched. "Moss was herding," he said. "It's what he's supposed to do."

What it was really all about, thought Jody, was that Moss had just now proved he was ready to go home.

23 Jody's mother was still out when Sharon dropped off Jody and Moss. "The coast's clear," she said as she handed him his wet sneakers with the socks stuffed inside them.

He had sat at Sharon's kitchen table in his father's pants and shirt while hamburgers and fries sizzled on the stove, and then he had changed back into his own things after Dad had left for work. Except for his jeans, the clothes he was wearing had dried out in the sun.

"Trouble is that dog's too clean," Sharon remarked as Moss jumped down from the cab.

Jody knew she was half kidding. He was worried, though. Moss's black and white coat looked shiny and soft. And his limp was more pronounced than usual. How would Jody be able to explain all this?

He raced barefoot to the door to get off the hot walk. Inside the house he padded to his room, put on dry jeans, fresh socks, and his outgrown sneakers, and carried his wet ones out to the yard to finish drying. There his eye fell on the hose. He could say that he had given Moss a bath. He had the wet leash to show for it. Maybe Moss had rolled in some crap. Not at Dad's, though. Jody didn't want Mom getting suspicious about Sharon and Dad doing stuff with Moss. Not after the kind of day they'd had, with Moss getting to do something he loved and Dad almost approving. Jody had come away feeling that Dad and Sharon were on Moss's side.

Not that Mom wasn't. Only she saw things differently.

When Jody heard the car drive up, he hurried back inside. But only Marie got out. Without a glance his way, she went striding to her door. Where was Mom?

He waited more than an hour. Then he went next door, startling his aunt.

"What are you doing home so early?" She didn't sound exactly thrilled to see him. "Brenda said you'd be gone all day."

"Dad got called out on a job." Jody didn't tell her he'd been home for a while. "Where's Mom?"

"She and Phil went out on an inspection."

"Where?" What was wrong with Aunt Marie? Did she mind that they had gone somewhere without her? "Inspecting what?"

"Calves," Aunt Marie told him. "The thing Phil's been looking into for a long time. Brenda needs, well, she was sort of losing her nerve, so she needed to be pumped up about something. So Phil's going to show her stuff."

Jody gave his aunt a blank look. He had no idea what she was talking about.

Aunt Marie said, "I brought a pizza home for you. I'm going out tonight."

"You mean Mom's not coming home?"

"They went up-country. They might stay over."

"Up-country?" Jody almost shouted. "Up-country, like where we were?"

Aunt Marie frowned. "You got a problem with that?"

"Of course I do," Jody told her. "How can she go all that way without Moss?"

"Laddie, not Moss. Lad."

"All right, Lad. He's well enough to go now. They should've taken him back—" Jody broke off. Moss had been with him at the reservoir, at Dad's. But Mom could have called and stopped by to pick up the dog.

"You don't get it, do you?" Aunt Marie said to him. "Your mom's been trying to break it to you as gently as possible, but you refuse to understand."

Jody felt clammy, as if he still had on all those drenched clothes. "What? What am I supposed to understand?"

"We can't take Lad back. Not now, not ever."

"We can!" Jody yelled. "He's fine now. I know he is."

"That's what Brenda was starting to think. That's why we're worried about her. Ever since that sheep rescue backfired, she's been wavering. She needs to be reminded what's at stake here, and so do you. If those people get Lad back all stitched up like he is, they'll start asking questions about who had him and why it took so long and stuff. They'll get in touch with all the vets for miles around. It wouldn't take long to track down the vet we went to. How many Border Collies got treated for those kind of wounds around the first weekend in May? Besides, the police can trace us through your mom's license."

"You can return him anyway. You can tell them you just found him and didn't know who he belonged to," Jody pleaded. "They won't blame anyone. They'll be grateful."

"Yeah, right. Grateful for about five minutes. Then they'll start thinking. Then they'll get so steamed they'll want to kill us. People are weird about their animals. They own them like slaves. They don't realize that animals have as much right to be free as we do."

"Free like those sheep you let out?" Jody blurted. "Free to get chased and killed?"

"So that's where Brenda's coming from," his aunt said. "She's been listening to you. And it sounds like you've been listening to your loudmouth father. You never used to talk like this. What's gotten into you?"

"Nothing," Jody replied, thinking: Moss. "Anyhow," he added, "Moss isn't free. He's our prisoner."

"You're right. But we'll find him a home where he can be free. Someplace with a big yard. He'll think he's died and gone to heaven."

Jody turned away from her and headed for the door. "He's in hell now," he muttered as he left for his side of the house.

But when he found Moss flat out on the kitchen floor and the cats spread out all over the place, it occurred to him that for a few minutes today Moss had actually been in sheepdog heaven. For the first time since he had been brought here, Moss looked like a dog that had worked hard and was enjoying a well-earned rest.

24 When Jody's mother returned Sunday afternoon, she couldn't stop talking about the pathetic calves she had seen, each one isolated in a small house and outdoor pen. "They should be kicking up their heels and playing with each other," she said. "They don't have their mothers, and they don't have playmates, and they'll be killed and turned into veal while they're still babies. I can see why Phil's a vegetarian."

She didn't notice that Moss looked extra clean. She didn't complain that Jody hadn't taken care of the cat boxes.

When finally he mumbled something about homework and

escaped to his room, she announced that she was going over to Marie's to tell her all about the farm animals.

But he didn't feel like doing homework. It hardly mattered anymore since school was practically finished. So he took Moss out for a second long walk, this time skirting the playground where earlier that day he had hung out for a while with Tara.

This time he wanted to be alone to think. If Mom hadn't come home all fired up about calf abuse, he might have been able to ask her about Moss's future before Aunt Marie had a chance to tell her about their argument. He felt stymied now. His aunt would beat him to the punch. Already he could feel her presence in his mother's heated jabber. It was weird the way Mom had rattled on and on, almost as if she were trying to fend off something else.

Fend off what? Was she keeping something from him?

He guessed that he'd better not bring up the subject of Moss with her, at least until he had some idea of what she had in mind. The important thing was to keep from stirring things up. He mustn't force her to take some action that might make it even harder to get Moss home.

He glanced at Moss trotting beside him. The dog seemed to look nowhere. He just went along, slightly favoring his game leg but still keeping pace with Jody. Making no waves, giving away nothing of himself. Biding his time.

That's how it's done, thought Jody. Like that. Like Moss.

Only how much time did they have? Maybe Jody needed to do something soon. If only he could call someone—Diane or Janet or the person who owned the farm that had hosted the sheepdog trial. If only he knew just one last name. He didn't even have a clue to who Moss's true owner was, even though he sort of remembered that Diane had mentioned a strange-sounding name.

The trouble with that kind of information was that you needed to realize it was crucial at the time you heard it. Otherwise it slipped past you and was lost in the jumble of impressions and fragments of conversation that had seemed unimportant at the time.

Jody stopped, an idea taking shape. He sat down against a tree, pondering. Moss stood facing him as if expecting a command.

"Lie down," Jody said.

Grunting, Moss circled and dropped, one paw landing on the toe of Jody's sneaker. It seemed a deliberate contact, perhaps a reminder that Moss was waiting to resume the walk. Or waiting to go home to Janet Something, who was probably still expecting Diane Something's best friend, name unknown, to come for the summer.

Jody groaned. How could he help Moss if he didn't know where he lived? Even if Jody took off on his own, he and Moss, he wouldn't know where to go or how to get there.

"But they know!" He had spoken out loud.

Moss raised his head and pressed his paw against the sneaker.

"Mom and Aunt Marie and Phil know where we were." Now he was actually addressing the dog. "I'm going to find out."

Moss dropped his chin on his leg, but his eyes were fastened on Jody's face.

"Come on," Jody declared, jumping to his feet. "We'll run all the way back." He hoped that would make up for the interrupted walk. Now that it had dawned on him there was something he might do, he couldn't wait to get started.

He arrived home breathless and buoyed with hope. First he

gave Moss a drink of water. Then he checked on Mom, who was down in the cellar starting a wash. Borrowing her car keys, he ran outside, opened the car door, and rummaged through the glove compartment until he came to a map of northern New England.

Back in the house he returned the car keys to the front table and took the map to his room, where he spread it out on his bed. Kneeling over it, he looked for the general area they had driven to that first weekend in May. But he wasn't used to reading maps. He couldn't figure distances. He had no idea how far they had driven that day. If only he had paid more attention.

When he heard Mom come up from the cellar, he folded the map and stuck it inside his school notebook. Then he joined her in the kitchen, where she was standing and gazing abstractedly at the open freezer compartment.

"What do you feel like having for supper," she asked him.

He shrugged. Then he said, "I had pizza last night. What did you have?"

"A good meal actually. In a restaurant near our motel."

"Anything like that motel we stayed at?" he asked her without actually trying to pin her down about where that had been.

"I guess they're all pretty much the same," she said. "At least the crummy ones up-country are. Unless you hit a resort. Which we didn't," she added. "Why? Does it bother you that Phil and I stayed together last night?"

He was so embarrassed that the next question flew right out of his head. "I don't care what we have," he told her.

"Fish sticks then," she decided, pulling a carton out and shutting the freezer door. "You finish your homework yet?"

"Almost," he answered, despairing of ever getting her to reveal what he needed to know.

But this had been only the first try, he told himself later on. Probably he should steer clear of Mom when it came to tracking down where they had been. Phil might be easier to get information out of. He didn't know Jody all that well, so he wasn't apt to get suspicious like Mom or Aunt Marie. Only that meant getting to him alone. How could Jody manage that?

On his way to his room he caught sight of Moss skulking behind the lounge chair. Sure enough, there was a cat in the chair. Slowly Moss approached, his eyes probing and intense. After a moment the cat jumped off the chair and retreated to the kitchen.

Moss scanned the living room until he was sure he had cleared the area. Then he took up his vigil at the front door.

25

The end of school was just one of many changes in Jody's life. Or maybe they just seemed to be changes because Jody was home most of every day to experience them. For one thing Mom was more absent, not just when she was at work but evenings, too. Even if she didn't go out at night, she was so preoccupied that certain things she might have dealt with before seemed to escape her entirely.

When Jody began to leave the cat boxes for her, she simply ignored them until the stench became so unbearable that even Phil and Aunt Marie complained. Then after another rescue, involving an emaciated cat and four kittens, Mom's friends succeeded in placing some of the older cats. For a little while the cat scene at home improved.

But ever since the goose gather in the reservoir, Moss's herding instinct seemed to have shifted into high gear. He worked the cats more often and more intensely, still silent, of course, and deaf to Mom's attempts to stop him. Aunt Marie pointed out that he wasn't actually doing any harm, but the constant stalking got on Mom's nerves.

Jody didn't know what to make of her edginess, so he tried to steer clear of her. That wasn't too hard. Even if she wasn't deliberately avoiding him, she didn't seek him out either. It was almost as if her irritability over Moss's behavior had spread to Jody.

"Why don't you two go out?" she would snap after managing to release the cats into her bedroom while shutting the door in Moss's face. "It's obvious he's not getting enough exercise."

Jody, who might already have spent several hours walking and jogging with Moss, would take off once again. These outings had finally brought him to the high school, where he began to be accepted by some of the regulars who worked out on the track. One guy, Sam Lynch, showed up with his dog, and the two of them raced Jody and Moss, who lost, though not by much.

Sam said, "I bet we could make good money running people's dogs for them," and they began to talk about putting up notices in local stores. They considered charging five dollars an hour. They thought they could probably handle two dogs at a time along with their own. It sounded like a good prospect to Jody, who kept thinking that unless he had some cash on hand, when a break came and he had a lead on where to take Moss, he wouldn't have any way of getting there.

Sam made flyers on his home computer. Jody showed one to Tara, who doubted whether anyone from their neighborhood would pay that much to get their dogs walked.

"You have to go to rich people," she said. "All those homes on the other side of town where everyone's loaded. And then they'll want references before they let their precious doggies out with strangers. For all they know, you're working for a dognapping ring."

Jody caught his breath. "Yeah. I didn't think of that." Which was true. It hadn't occurred to him that anyone might think him capable of stooping so low. He wished he could just spill his guts to her right here, right now. He looked at Tara. She wasn't so bad, really. They had some laughs together with the little kids. And now that school was out, things were easier between them. But he didn't know how to get past everything he had kept from her up to now. He could imagine how he'd feel if he discovered that someone he was getting to know had been lying to him since day one.

So he kept his mouth shut. Instead he talked about Sam, who might be able to dig up some references. But all the time he spoke, he could feel that easy money slipping away before he had even earned it.

He redoubled his efforts to close in on Moss's home turf. Thinking that if he came across a printed place-name, it might jog his memory, he went over the road map town by town. But nothing rang a bell. He made a list of everything he knew, which consisted of only two first names and one whole one: Diane, Janet, Billy Mount. So he made a longer list of things he needed to find out: Diane's last name and her hometown, Janet's last name and hometown, the place where the sheepdog trial was held, the location of the motel they stayed in. Finally he made a third list, this time of towns that had a slightly familiar ring to their names: Madison (but maybe he was thinking of Wisconsin),

Canterbury (it could almost be the place Diane had mentioned), Pittsfield (only the one he knew, where his grandparents lived, was in Massachusetts).

Then a thought struck him. The forklift driver had mentioned a sheepdog trial at a fair in a place called Chiswick. That sent Jody back to the map in search of Chiswick. But it wasn't there. Had he spelled it wrong? Heard it wrong? Even if he found it, what then? Would Janet be likely to go there?

He jumped up, not even bothering to fold the map, just shoving it with the list under his bed. He found Moss eyeing the heap of cats on the couch. Only the kittens would not stay put. They kept tumbling onto the floor and attacking Moss's tail or chasing each other around his paws. This only made him back off so that he could include them in his stare and nudge them toward the couch. With the kittens to control, his job was never done.

"Come on," Jody told him. "That'll do, here."

With a sidelong glance at his feline flock, Moss went to Jody and stood to be leashed. They didn't usually go out in the heat of the day, but Jody couldn't wait. He wanted to find the forklift driver while he was still at work.

But it was too hot to jog all the way through the park and over the hill and along the tracks. Because they had to alternate walking and running, it took them more than an hour to reach the warehouse. Jody was drenched with sweat; Moss's tongue lolled and dripped. There was the forklift. But the loading area seemed deserted.

Jody approached but didn't mount the platform. Instead he went around to the long, windowless side of the building. There was one door, dwarfed by the immensity of the blank wall. Jody tried knocking before he opened the door and looked in. A few men were lounging against the inside of the wall and sitting on stacks of pallets.

"You looking for somebody?" one of them inquired.

Jody nodded. He didn't even know whom to ask for.

But a man detached himself from the group. "It's the sheepdog boy," he said.

Jody nodded again. In the cool dimness of the warehouse, under the blue light of fluorescent ceiling tubes, he would never have recognized this man.

"You been running again," the man remarked. "You should go easy on a day like this. Take a break like we do." He turned on a hose and rinsed out a hubcap, which he then filled and offered to Moss. Moss lapped up all the water and flopped down on the concrete floor.

The man turned to Jody. "You want a Coke or something?"

Jody started to say no thanks but then nodded instead. One of the other men handed over a drink from a cooler. Jody thanked him. He gulped down half the contents of the can before he spoke again. Then he told the forklift driver he had come to find out the name of the place with the fair that had the sheepdog trial. He wanted to go there. He needed the date, too.

The forklift driver told him the fair was in Chiswick. It was one of the earliest fairs of the season, starting on the Friday before the second weekend in August. The trial was on Saturday.

"And do a lot of dogs run in it?" Jody asked him.

"I believe so. And not just from Maine. They come from all over, New Hampshire, Vermont, New York. There's some from Canada, too."

Maine! "Chiswick's in Maine?" Jody exclaimed.

"Of course," the driver replied. "Where I come from. I told you, didn't I?"

"Oh," said Jody. "I guess I missed that part. How long to get there?"

The driver considered. "Depends on the traffic. Maybe three hours. Even if you make good time on the interstate, you can lose half of it just getting into one of the parking fields. Your folks taking you? Better warn them. People near the fairgrounds rent parking on their lawns. It's worth it just to be there."

He refilled the hubcap and offered it to Moss. "You should take the dog. Let him see what his relatives can do."

Jody almost blurted that Moss could work sheep, too. Instead he said, "Maybe we'll see you there. Thanks a lot."

"No problem," the driver said. "Take it easy."

The men were already drifting away to their jobs. Jody let himself out into the blinding sunshine. Eager as he was to pinpoint Chiswick on the map, he let Moss set a pace through the afternoon heat. As they plodded along, he mulled over the biggest hurdle, getting Moss to the fair on that weekend without Mom or Aunt Marie or any of the others. Even if he did make some money between now and then, there was no way he could persuade a bus driver to take him and a dog to Chiswick or the nearest place to it that a bus might go.

26 Poring over the road map seemed more productive now. As soon as Jody found Chiswick in Maine, he began to apply himself all over again to the search for names that might jog his memory. This time one place jumped out at him as if it had a life of its own: Coventry. Maybe that was why he had singled out Canterbury in New Hampshire. The two names sounded sort of alike.

He was almost certain that Diane had mentioned it. Where she lived? Where Janet lived? Or did he simply connect it with Diane because it was where the sheepdog trial was held?

"Remember when we were in Maine?" he said to Phil in what he hoped was an offhand way. They were sweltering in the van as they waited for Mom and Aunt Marie.

"We were in Maine?" Phil said testily. "When was that?"

"You know, up-country, where we got . . . Lad."

"That was New Hampshire," Phil told him. He leaned out the window and shouted, "Brenda! Marie!"

Bingo! thought Jody. Things were falling into place. "I thought it was Maine," he continued, "because some of those dog people live there."

"Nope. Close, though. Anyway, what about it?" Phil's fingers tapped the steering wheel.

"I was just thinking," Jody said, stalling while he tried to come up with something that wouldn't arouse Phil's suspicion.

"Finally!" Phil exclaimed as Jody's mother and aunt came rushing out of the house.

Aunt Marie said they had plenty of time. She had already scoped out the place, and parking was no problem. "Westwick's like country," she said.

"Can we bring Lad?" Jody asked. "He'd like the country."

They hesitated. Then Mom said, "Why not? It might get his mind off the cats."

"But he'll make us more noticeable," Phil objected.

"Not us. Jody. So it'll be easier for him to distract people."

Jody dashed back to get Moss. He had no idea what he was supposed to do on this mission. He guessed that Mom had been vague to keep him from digging in his heels and refusing to help. She hadn't caught on yet to his new cooperative attitude. Maybe after today she would pick up on it. Of course that would depend on how well he carried off his side of things. He needed to bear in mind that it was important for them to believe that he no longer opposed them.

When he opened the window for Moss, who leaned out to feel the moving air, traffic noise prevented his hearing what the three up front were discussing. So he just sat back and watched the passing scene, first the streets like his with small divided houses and triple-deckers, then stores, then buildings for larger businesses, until the van reached the heart of the city, hemmed in by tractor trailers and panel trucks and vans and cars, all in a hurry, all clogging the streets.

Moss recoiled from the noise and fumes and settled down beside Jody, his head turned from the outside world. He stayed that way until they finally made it to the turnpike and headed out of the city. Once they were on smaller roads, Moss was alert again, his eyes seeking what he could not see, his nostrils quivering as if testing familiar smells.

By the time they reached the town of Westwick, he was pressing at the window. Jody guessed that all the fields and woods they passed made Moss think he was nearing home. "Soon," Jody promised, his whisper muffled against the dog.

They had to walk from the school parking lot across a meadow and along what looked like a country road. Most of the people knew the way. Some lugged kids in wagons, some carried babies in backpacks, and on every side children ran and yelled back and forth, many of them slowing to pat Moss as they passed.

Even with his uneven gait, there was a spring to his step. His manner was grave as always, but he wagged his tail at oncoming kids. Once again Jody was reminded that Moss had lived with Janet's two small boys.

If Mom and the other adults noticed Moss's response, they didn't comment on it. They were planning their strategy for rescuing the frogs, Marie pointing to the small pond along the road they had to cross.

"Frogs?" Jody exclaimed. He couldn't believe what he was finally able to hear.

"Ssh!" Aunt Marie cautioned. "Don't attract attention. Yet."

Ahead under balloons strung between trees hung a sign reading: WELCOME TO WESTWICK COMMUNITY FAIR. When they stopped at the gate to buy tickets, they were given a program of events with a small map. Everything—sign, program, and map—had been made by kids.

Mom shook her head. "Where did you hear about this?" she said to Phil. "It's all homemade stuff. Can we really come in here and spoil it for them?"

"You bet we can," Aunt Marie told her. "They may not mean any harm, but they still need their consciousness raised."

"Brenda," Phil said, his arm around Mom's shoulders, "we're not spoiling all of it. Anyway, it was announced on one of those radio spots for weekend activities in and out of the city."

Moss yearned toward a fence with another homemade sign: OLD MACDONALD'S FARM. Small children accompanied by parents could go pet the goat and lambs and feed bread to the ducks that paddled in a wading pool. Moss crouched, his eyes riveted on the animals.

"Look at the sheepdog," one man said. "I guess he knows what he was born for."

"Get him away from here," Mom whispered to Jody. "Don't let him do that."

Jody had to tell Moss, "That'll do," four times before he would unlock his gaze and be led away.

The fair consisted mostly of kids' games, a flea market that was really like a huge yard sale, lots of food booths with lemonade and homemade bread and brownies and sandwiches, and special events.

One special event, the frog race, had been targeted by Phil and Aunt Marie for disruption. They had come to end the exploitation of the frogs. Mom had come for the same reason; only she lacked the others' conviction.

"If they're not hurt—" she tried to argue.

"Look at what they're forced to do," Phil interrupted. "They can be hurt if they're poked to keep them going in the right direction."

"Besides," Aunt Marie added, "it says that only kids who have caught their own frogs can enter. You know what that means? A lot of squeezing and worse."

Jody looked at the racecourse, which was like a miniature track with lanes chalked in white lime. As a small crowd gathered, a man announced that only six frogs at a time could compete. The winners of each race would then have a second chance.

Jody saw Phil and Aunt Marie size up the situation. Boxes with holes punched in them and buckets with screening over the top were left in the shade of a large maple tree to keep cool. The frogs' owners, on the other hand, crowded around the course to see how the others were doing. That left the waiting boxes and buckets unattended.

"Quick," Phil ordered, producing white plastic bags and a sheaf of papers with something printed on them. "Jody, you stand there and stop anyone heading this way."

"How?" asked Jody.

Phil gave him a look. "It doesn't matter how. Use the dog."

Jody kept turning partway to watch Phil scoop up one frog

Jody remembered this man now. He was the one who had seen Moss eyeing the goat and lambs and had said something about what sheepdogs were born for.

For one split second Jody came close to appealing to him for help. It was a dangerous impulse, since it could lead to some outsider's taking over the dog. How could a stranger begin to understand the urgency of getting Moss home?

Jody must trust no one.

27 Back together in the van the three adults were in high spirits. It felt good when everything went as planned. Jody in the back said nothing.

"No hitches," said Phil, "unless we count the frogs we couldn't get hold of."

Aunt Marie turned to Jody. "What happened when they found the others gone?"

"Someone asked if Moss ate them," he said.

"You're kidding!" Mom sounded shocked as well as disgusted.

"It was a joke," Jody told her.

"They made jokes about a dog eating pet frogs?"

"Not exactly," he said. "I guess you had to be there."

"I'm glad you were," Aunt Marie said to him. "It's good to have you on our team again. Maybe we can get you to pitch in on a really big mission."

"Not now," Mom said in an undertone.

"Why not?" Aunt Marie retorted. "He's going to hear about it sooner or later."

"Marie's right," Phil chimed in. "This was frills compared to what's coming next."

They said nothing else about it then. Jody was in no hurry to hear more. He dreaded being dragged along on another of their missions. Yet he didn't dare give them a hard time about it. Maybe he should pretend that he might still be bribed with the prospect of a favorite meal.

But when Phil stopped at an ice-cream stand and Aunt Marie remarked that Jody usually needed more of a meal than that, Mom said this would be fine. Lately she'd noticed that the heat did a number on Jody's appetite, same as everyone else. When she turned to him for confirmation, he was quick to agree, even though secretly he worried that any day now Phil would win her over and she would stop buying hamburgers and fried chicken altogether. Jody wasn't ready to deal with that. With an image to maintain, he ordered a super sundae. Mom caught him sharing it with Moss and reminded him that chocolate is bad for dogs. So Moss only got some of the ice cream and whipped topping.

Phil dropped them off at home. Jody's mother lingered a moment with him before following Jody to the house. Aunt Marie had already gone in her door.

Inside, the cats thudded to the floor from their various perches and the kittens scampered over to Moss. When one of them tried to climb his game leg, he growled softly, which prompted Jody's mother to say, "No, no," to Moss and, "That reminds me," to Jody.

Why did he have the feeling that she had something on her mind that didn't need reminding? Something to do with Phil?

"Are you going out later?" he asked, trying to fend off whatever it was that made her sound so phony.

"Maybe. Yes. We're going to the movies."

Jody nodded. "We" of course meant Mom and Phil. So Jody could let Moss herd the cats and banish them all to Mom's room.

"They want me to tell you about what's coming down. That mission. And what it means for us here."

Jody plumped down on the couch. This wasn't so bad then. She wasn't announcing that Phil was like moving in or anything.

"There's a dog that's used to guard stuff. It's a fenced lot for RVs and lawn mowers and garden tractors, things like that, and it's out a ways. Phil took me to see the dog there, no water, no shade, except what he can find beside the skimobile he's chained to. I couldn't get near him. He's real aggressive, which is what they want him to be. At night they let him loose in the lot. Phil thinks we can get him out. You should see him, Jody. He's covered with sores and—"

"What about the Humane Society? Can't they do something about it?"

Mom shook her head. "They investigated. You know how it is. They come, and a water bowl miraculously appears beside the dog, who is moved to the open bay of a shed. No, the abuse will go on unless he's rescued."

It sounded like a real case of need. How could Jody object to helping? He let her see that he was sympathetic to this cause.

That was when she dropped the bombshell. Leaning toward him, she said, "It means we'll have to move Moss on."

He held his breath. She was telling him that it was over. Moss would be home where he belonged. Diane and her friend would find out that he was all right after all. He might even get to run in that sheepdog trial in Chiswick.

Mom said, "As long as Lad is here, we can't bring the other dog in. We have no way to isolate him if he has some contagious condition. Besides, he could be vicious with other dogs. As it is, we'll have to separate the cats, at least at first. He's nothing like Lad. Do you understand?"

Jody nodded. "And he's ready. He really is. When can we take him?"

"I'm not sure exactly. Soon. So far I've got one very good prospect."

What did she mean, prospect? "Did you find out where Janet lives?"

That brought his mother up short. "Janet?" She stared at him, then shook her head. "No. Oh, no, Jody, we can't do that. It's impossible."

"No, it isn't. There's a way to—"

"There isn't any way to return him without going back to the trial farm and asking questions. Anything we do to get him to his old home will leave us exposed. That would finish us. That would mean that animals like this desperate dog I've been telling you about will never be saved. How can we risk all our future missions for this?"

"You have to," Jody cried. "Moss is theirs. They're probably still hunting for him. How would you feel?"

"I am sorry," she said. "Really I am. I wish we could get him home. I know he's unhappy. Don't you think I see that?"

"Then do something about him. Try," Jody pleaded. "Think of Janet. Think of Diane and her friend that owns Moss. She was coming all the way from California to be with him this summer."

"If she loves him so much," Mom asked, "why doesn't she keep him with her?"

"Because," Jody declared. "Because he's a sheepdog. He was born to work. He was trained to work. That's what he needs."

Mom shook her head. "What's wrong with that picture, Jody? Think what happens to him if he can't handle sheep anymore? Do you know how many of those people sell their dogs when they don't work out for them? I kept hearing about that at the trial. They just move them along to make room for dogs they can win with. What about responsibility and bonding and companionship?"

Jody was stumped. "All I know is how bad Diane felt."

Mom shook her head again. "It's crummy. But at least we'll see that Lad has a good home where he'll be loved."

"Don't call him Lad," Jody stormed at her.

Mom frowned. "He has a new life now. He has a new name. I know this is hard on you," she went on, her tone softened. "You've done a great job with Lad. I'm sure you'll miss him."

He said, "If there was a way to get him back to Janet without being found out, would you do it?"

"I— Yes. I'd try. If I could be sure she'd keep him." She sighed. "The problem is it's not just up to me. Marie and Phil are in on this, too. They don't want to go near those people, directly or indirectly. It's too risky."

"Don't you have the right to do what you think should be done?"

She reached toward him, but he drew back. "I have a right, yes," she told him. "But I also have a lot to lose if I screw up."

"Because Aunt Marie's your sister?" Then what about your son? he wondered, but not out loud.

"Because of Phil, too. We're in this together. There was a point when I thought . . . I almost wanted out. Then Phil and I . . . got close. Now the situation's changed. I can't just do what I'd like to do unless I want to go it alone. All the way. Do you see?"

Jody saw. Phil wasn't moving in. Yet. But he had taken over in a way that affected Jody as much as moving in or marrying Mom.

Jody couldn't meet her eyes. "I see," he mumbled, knowing that he sounded defeated and almost feeling that way.

But not quite. Time might be running out for Moss, but there was no way that Jody was giving up on him. Not now, when that sheepdog trial was drawing close.

28 With August looming, time pressed in on Jody from either side. That fair trial seemed to him the only chance he had to locate Janet and get Moss home where he belonged. Meanwhile the dog savers chafed to get on with their big mission.

But first Moss had to be placed.

Early every morning Jody took off with him and didn't return until Mom and Aunt Marie had left for work. Late in the afternoon he ran again, usually meeting up with Sam. When they got bored with the track, they went cross-country. Sam was in better shape, but Jody, who pursued him as though possessed, was seldom far behind.

"Hey, Jody, chill, will you?" Sam told him. "You'll make the team."

Between gasps, Jody could only shake his head and mutter, "Getting . . . Moss . . . fit." He couldn't explain that running felt like getting somewhere, like progress. He couldn't admit that he was afraid of blowing up at his mother or Aunt Marie. It was easier to stay out of their way than to act resigned like Moss. After all, even Moss's rebel spirit took over whenever he stalked the cats.

Jody slipped only once. It happened when his mother let him

know that Moss's adoption was on hold until the family she had in mind returned from a vacation in the White Mountains. He couldn't help asking why Phil or someone else didn't take the guard dog, at least for a while. Patiently Mom explained to him that she was the only one of them who knew how to treat a dog with medical problems, and she was the only one with a private backyard where a dog could be safe from discovery. "As for the rest of the group," she went on, "you know we never divulge specifics to each other. It's the only way we can protect ourselves in case someone gets in trouble."

"You mean, busted?" Jody said in spite of his determination not to challenge her.

"You know what I mean. If somebody gets caught, it'll knock that one person out of commission, but it needn't be the end for the rest of us. Our work can go on."

He felt like asking: Even if you don't agree with what's going down? But he managed to keep his mouth shut. He couldn't afford to oppose her, especially when he was bound to lose to Phil. Right now, with Mom all fired up about this guard dog, Phil and Aunt Marie had the upper hand. Even Jody couldn't find fault with that rescue.

Afterward he mulled over what Mom had told him. Was there a way to screw up somehow so that Moss would have to be removed from the house to protect the others? Maybe that was how he could get Mom to consider trying to return Moss to Janet. Jody warmed to this idea. If he managed things just right, he might not only force Mom's hand about Moss but knock himself out of commission, too.

Only the more he thought about it, the more he worried about putting Moss at greater risk. What if Marie or Phil or both of them talked Mom into disposing of Moss another way? They might convince her to resort to a different adoption. That danger seemed so real to Jody that it stopped him cold.

He was on his way home from the high school track when his father's pickup slowed beside him, Sharon at the wheel. She offered him and Moss a lift home.

"Should you be working out so hard when it's this hot?" she asked, casting her eyes over his sweat-drenched T-shirt. "You're not overdoing it, are you?"

As Moss jumped into the cab, Jody felt again her easiness with the dog. Sharon didn't touch Moss, and he didn't seek her attention. But the look he gave her as he settled down at Jody's feet reminded him of the way Moss recognized Tara whenever they met. If it wasn't exactly trust, at least it came close to a kind of acceptance.

Jody drew a deep breath. In a flash he saw a solution to his predicament. But it required something like Moss's near trust.

When he finally spoke, Sharon could barely hear him. "What?" She rolled up her window. "What did you say?"

"If Moss might be in some kind of danger," he repeated, "would you and Dad be able to keep him for a few days?"

"What kind of danger?" she asked. Then quickly she added, "Never mind. I don't want to know."

They were stopped at a red light. She glanced over at Jody and then down at the dog. She shook her head. She said, "Your dad wants nothing to do with . . . you know." She paused. "Still, I suppose this is different. I'll talk to him. He knows the dog means a lot to you."

She rolled down her window, and nothing more was said until she dropped Jody off and he thanked her.

"Get a shower," she told him with a smile. "I don't know which smells worse, you or the dog."

He grinned back at her. "Moss is his real name," Jody said, "but they call him Lad. Okay?"

"Got it," Sharon told him as she pulled away from the curb.

Moss drank so much water that Jody took him out back to pee before going in to shower. He was still in the bathroom when his mother got home from work. He hurried out and found her collapsed in front of the fan.

"You look cool," she said enviously

"I thought the animal hospital was air-conditioned," he said.

She nodded. "It's leaving there that gets me. The contrast." She looked at him. "It's so hot Lad isn't even bothering the cats. Maybe that's why they call this part of the summer dog days. Are you very hungry?"

He shook his head. "Only thirsty." He knew she didn't want to stir. This was the time to make his move.

"Good," she said. "Me, too."

He said, "I'd still go for something salty, fries or chips or something." He groped for the right words, the right tone. "Lad drank like a gallon when we got home. Made me think about that guard dog without water." He paused to let that much sink in. "If you guys decide to get him out of that place as soon as possible, maybe Dad and Sharon could, like, take care of Lad. You know, just for a few days."

Mom shook her head. "I don't think so. Your father hates what I do."

"Yeah, maybe. But last visit we had a good time with Moss. We went to the reservoir." Cool it, Jody told himself. Don't push her.

Silence fell. Was she dismissing the idea? Was she considering? Finally she spoke. "He'd never do it. He wouldn't do anything for me."

"What about me?" Jody asked. "You think he wouldn't do it for me either?"

His mother shrugged. "You want to find out?"

"I can try," Jody told her. "Can't hurt to try." He walked into the kitchen to look for something cold to drink. Moss, sprawled on his back against the screen door, shifted only slightly as Jody swooped down to hug him. "We're on our way," Jody whispered, "on our way."

29

Every day grew hotter, and every evening thunder rolled across the distant sky. At the first rumbling Moss would start to pant, his eyes darting from one shadow to another, his ears flat against his head.

The night CAATS met at Jody's house, the storm finally erupted over the city. First the lights flickered and the television crackled. Then heavy raindrops splattered on the windowsill.

Moss pushed open Jody's door and crawled into the closet. At the same time the voices in the living room rose as if charged by all the energy released into the air.

Until then Jody hadn't realized that they were discussing the urgent need for foster homes for rescued animals. He left his door open so that he could catch any reference to Moss.

The question was whether it would be safe to bring in people who might not agree with the group's rescue tactics, enlisting the aid of such people without telling them exactly how the animals had been obtained. Jody's mother objected. She thought it would be wrong to involve anyone in breaking the law without their knowledge and consent.

"If it's the only way to save an abused animal?" Aunt Marie demanded.

"There's got to be another way," Jody's mother retorted as lightning cast Jody's room in an eerie white glare.

Was she talking about Moss going to Dad and Sharon? Jody had no idea how Aunt Marie and Phil felt about that plan. When Jody had put down the phone after speaking to Sharon and had informed his mother that it would be okay for a day or so, Mom had sounded both relieved and anxious. Later on she had cautioned Jody against mentioning it anymore. "The less said, the better," was how she had put it.

Probably Aunt Marie hated the idea of Dad's having anything to do with Moss. She knew that he called her and Mom Thelma and Louise. Aunt Marie usually referred to him as "that lowlife."

A tremendous thunderclap silenced everyone in the living room. Then they all started talking at once, and all Jody could hear was a general babble. Soon even that was drowned out as Moss dug away at the closet floor. Shoes and a lost sock shot into the room.

Jody dived down beside Moss, who seemed determined to make a hole in the floor and climb into it. Deaf to Jody's words of comfort, the dog buried his head under Jody's arm and kept it there. Shudders ran through his body long after the thunder had died away.

What if there was a storm while Moss was with Dad and Sharon? In a panic he might squeeze out the door and take off. Dad and Sharon would never get him back. Jody ought to warn them to keep the dog confined if there was thunder. Would Jody be pushing his luck if he recommended that they practice commands like "stay" and "that'll do, come"?

Slowly Moss relaxed. Slowly Jody released him. He was going to need a clear head. Once the mission was under way and he was taking his cue from Mom and Phil and Aunt Marie, he couldn't let this kind of worry distract him, because he might not know until almost the last minute just how he was going to turn things around.

After the meeting broke up, Mom and Aunt Marie and Phil went into the kitchen and closed the door. They stayed there a long time, their voices in the low, conspiratorial register that often meant they were in the final phase of planning.

Before going to bed, Jody took Moss out the front way for a pee. The ground was saturated from the recent downpour. It must have given off a whole new range of scents, because Moss took his time, sniffing even where there was only asphalt and refuse at a drain. Would Dad or Sharon think of taking Moss for a late-night outing? Maybe sending him over there would be a mistake.

The moment Jody came into the house he felt the charged atmosphere in the living room, where they were waiting for him.

"We expect you to play by the rules," Phil told him. "Your part is vital."

Did Phil mean now? It was too soon. The fair was more than a week off.

"We'll go over this again, but we think you should be prepared."

Jody nodded. "When?" he asked.

"We don't know exactly," Mom said. "Phil's been over to that lot almost every night this week. He'll pick the right time."

"It'll take three of us to restrain the dog," Phil said.

"How come?"

"He's trained to attack. I'm going to cut a few toeholds in the fence so you can climb it. Then I'll cut a larger hole farther along the fence, big enough for the dog to get his head through. We'll have a noose to go around his neck. We'll cross-tie him. Marie and I will be on opposite sides pulling hard enough so that Brenda will be able to get a restraining muzzle on him."

"Isn't that rough on the dog?" Jody asked.

"You can say that again," Aunt Marie snapped. "Major stress."

"That's why we have to be so quick about it," Phil went on. "There's an electronic security system for the storefront and office, but it doesn't affect the gate. While we immobilize the dog, you'll be going over to open the gate from the inside. One of us will have to hold on to the muzzled dog through the fence while two of us go around and through the gate to bring him out."

"Don't forget the money," Mom said.

"Oh, please!" Aunt Marie exclaimed. "First you refuse to give the dog a tranquilizing shot and then you worry about the guy's property?"

"I told you," Mom shot back, "tranquilizing's tricky. We don't know how much this dog weighs or anything else about his condition. Anyway, that has nothing to do with paying for the damage to the fence."

"Okay, Brenda, okay," Phil said. "We'll leave money. Jody, you can do that while we deal with the dog."

"How?" he asked. "Where?"

Phil said, "I'll have all the details mapped out before we go in. You just be on the ball."

Jody nodded. Of course he would go along with this plan. His own plan depended on it. But he wished he knew more about the security system.

Lying in bed that night, Jody went over his possible options. The trouble was that he couldn't picture the setup Phil had mentioned. Most of the movies he knew where electronic security devices were neutralized or tripped were set in the future, the systems more sophisticated than anything that was likely to be installed in a place that relied on a guard dog.

Was Jody getting in too deep? Should he bail out of this mission and just take off with Moss? But if he did, how could he count on hitching rides for the two of them that would get him to the Chiswick fair before he was picked up by the police? No, he had to stick with the guard dog rescue. At least if things didn't work out, Moss might still have a chance some other way.

No matter how it played, though, it was clear to Jody that he wouldn't be able to carry out the final phase of the return by himself.

Now that it was coming down to the crunch, Jody realized that he had already begun to count on others for help. How far could he trust Sharon and Dad? Jody didn't know. Nor was he sure just where his mother stood. Slippery ground, he thought. He would have to watch his step. If things looked bad, maybe he could still change his mind.

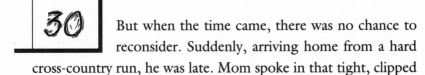 But when the time came, there was no chance to reconsider. Suddenly, arriving home from a hard cross-country run, he was late. Mom spoke in that tight, clipped

voice that usually went with all the missions he was dragged into. "We'll drop Lad off. Call them."

"Now?" he asked, alarmed. Why had she sprung it on him this way? "Where are the others?"

"On their way."

But there was no answer at his dad's. Jody had counted on having Moss safely over there before the guard dog rescue was launched. "Phone's busy," he lied to his mother. "I'll try again in a few minutes."

"No," she snapped. "We have to get started."

"I'll get my stuff," he said, trying to stall for time

"What stuff?"

"My knapsack. You always want me to have my knapsack in case it has to look like I'm stealing."

"Not this time," she told him.

He hurried into the kitchen, filled Moss's bowl, and set it down for him.

"Jody!" She was at the door.

"We've been running. He's thirsty."

Moss lapped eagerly. Even though Mom could tell he was thirsty, waiting was an ordeal for her. Jody had never seen her so tense.

After he tried calling Dad and Sharon again, Mom refused to be put off any longer. If the line was busy, then someone must be home. They would swing by on their way.

"Dog food!" he cried.

"I've got it," she said. "Come on."

In the car he asked, "What if they went out?"

"You mean, since you tried to call them?" Her tone was sharp. Was she beginning to doubt him?

"They might've," he said lamely. It was his best shot. He couldn't exactly back down.

As they approached his father's, he saw that the pickup wasn't there. But lights were on inside.

"Make it quick," Mom told him, handing him a bag of dog food.

Sharon kept him standing a long time before opening the door. Looking past her into the kitchen, he saw that she was doing someone's hair.

"I tried to call you," he said hurriedly.

"That was you? I was busy with a client." She tilted her head toward the kitchen.

"I'm sorry. We got back from running. There was no warning."

"So I can smell," she said, wrinkling her nose.

He handed her a leash. "Is it okay?" he asked.

"You tell me," she replied. Then, seeing how torn he was, she added, "Me and the dog, we'll be fine."

His mother beeped the horn.

"I don't guess you know when you'll be back for him?" Sharon asked.

"Not exactly," Jody said, "but could you save some time for this coming weekend in case we need to—to go somewhere? I'll explain . . . later."

She hesitated. "You want me to ask your father?"

He nodded. "Could you? Oh, thanks, Sharon, thanks."

Mom beeped again, and he ran back to the car. He had forgotten to tell Sharon the commands. He hadn't shown her how much to feed Moss. He had left him there without a word or a touch. Not now, he told himself, slamming the car door. Don't think of that now.

Mom took off with a lurch. They had to go through a part of

the city that emptied out at night. They passed the street where Jody's father worked. Dad earned overtime driving the machine shop's truck. If he were called out to work this coming weekend, would he turn down a job just because Jody had asked him to save the weekend?

On the expressway Mom picked up speed. She switched on the car radio and began to sing along with Bonnie Raitt. Jody leaned back. Singing always calmed Mom's nerves.

But as soon as the car was on the exit ramp, the radio and Mom shut down. She glanced at her watch. There was a long light at an intersection with gas stations on three of the corners. Then, after a brief stretch of empty lots, she turned in at a mostly darkened shopping center.

Phil's van was parked along with a few other vehicles at the side of a liquor store. Mom pulled in next to him. Jody knew the drill. The moment Mom opened her door, he got out on his side. Without a word they climbed inside the van.

"All set?" Phil asked as soon as they were on the main road.

"Jody?" Marie prompted. "Phil's speaking to you."

"Yep," Jody said. How was he supposed to know the question was for him?

"Okay," Phil told him, "there's a few things we all need to keep in mind. I've been watching the place. The security setup has a sensor that only kicks in at a certain level. Like the dog doesn't set it off. So anyone going near the building, stay low and don't touch anything that could be wired."

"Like what?" Jody's mother asked. "Jody's got to leave the printout and money."

"Like doors and windows," Phil said. He paused. "Maybe we should leave the envelope at the gate. Take our chances on it not blowing away."

"No way," Mom said. "That's my money you're talking about. Besides, the owner needs our message. If you don't think Jody should deal with it, I will."

Jody held his breath. His plan depended on his getting all the way to the building, but he knew better than to let on that he cared about delivering the envelope.

Phil parked near a discount tile store across the road from the RV lot. He had the bolt cutter in his hand and another tool in his pocket. Marie had the noose, Mom a muzzle shaped like a cone. Where was the envelope? Jody didn't dare ask.

Even after they had crossed over to the fenced lot, he had trouble seeing much beyond the first line of campers facing the road. The silence was so profound that for a moment he suspected it was all a mistake and there was no dog to be saved. But as soon as the bolt cutters bit through the first link in the fence, the dog shot forward from between two campers and lunged at the invading tool. Snarling and biting at the fence, it looked all jaws and teeth. Even in the semidark, sores were visible on its massive head.

"Won't someone hear him?" Jody whispered to his mother.

"People are used to it. Phil's been stirring him up other nights."

"Get his attention," Phil said as the dog snapped at the cutter. "I'm afraid I'll hurt him or he'll hurt himself."

Mom dragged the muzzle along the links and lured the dog from Phil. That worked long enough to let Phil cut out the upper toehold. He called softly to Jody to ask if that would do, or did Jody need more holes?

Jody said he guessed that would be enough.

"No guessing," Phil retorted. "It's now or never. Once I cut out the big hole for the dog, there'll be no going back here."

Jody looked more closely and nodded. "Okay," he said. "I'm cool."

"Now keep the dog over here," Phil ordered as he ran past Mom and Aunt Marie to begin opening up the fence for the headlock. Jody found a bent piece of reinforcing rod. He supposed he could use it to distract the dog. But he got more of a reaction than he'd bargained for. The moment he shoved the bar through the lower toehold, the dog attacked it. A strange, savage tug-of-war ensued, the dog gurgling as it tried to pull the rod out of Jody's grip.

Phil grunted as he cut through each link. The steel popped like muted gunshots. They seemed to Jody to go on and on. After that Phil used a vise grip to bend any prongs that might injure the dog. Then he was rubbing his hands and shaking them.

"Ready," Phil called softly. "Leave the dog alone now. We want him over here."

"He won't let go," Jody said.

"You do it," Phil told him. "Push it all the way through and drop it."

It unnerved Jody that he hadn't been able to think of that on his own. The moment the reinforcing rod came free, the dog resumed its barking. That rattled Jody even more. He joined Phil and Mom and Aunt Marie at the big hole. The dog ran along the other side of the fence and quickly found its way into the opening, but not out of it. Even so, no one could get the noose past those snapping jaws until Jody thought to replay the rod maneuver with a piece of strapping he picked off the ground. Although it splintered at the dog's first bite, it gave Phil the few seconds he needed to rope the dog and tighten the noose.

Mom said, "Jody, get over the fence."

"You don't need help with the muzzle?"

She shook her head. "Hurry!"

He had one foot lodged in place when she came rushing after him. "Here," she said, stuffing an envelope into his back pocket. "First the gate so we can get the dog through. Then this envelope. Leave it where it won't be missed. Don't forget what Phil told you. Oh, and remember to close the gate. Anyone driving by that knows this place would notice if it was left open."

Jody nodded. She was gone. He went on up, stabbing at the fence with his sneakered foot as he sought the upper hole from which he could boost himself over the top.

31 Being inside the lot on his own was like dropping into a different continuum. Maybe he had been reading too many space stories, but he couldn't help feeling weightless. And utterly alone. The others struggling with the dog were as distant as Sharon in her beauty parlor kitchen miles away. His head seemed to be stuffed with alien matter, something that absorbed all sound and blotted out the known world. Gate, he told himself as a robot might recite its program. Gate. Envelope.

Even though he ran to the gate, it took him a long time to reach it. Then his fingers wouldn't obey. They seemed to be frozen into the crooked hooks they had become while they had clung to the chain-link fence. The metal was cold and resistant. He broke into a sweat until it came to him that he wasn't trapped here. He could always climb back out the way he had come. But it struck him as odd that if he failed to open the gate, the others on the outside might be stuck, attached to that dog through the fence.

Then the latch yielded, and he was able to drag the gate inward. In the next instant Phil appeared. "Here," he said to Jody, thrusting the bolt cutter into his hands. "Take this." He sprinted along the inside of the fence toward the dog, whose muzzled head, held by Mom and Aunt Marie, was still lodged in the hole.

Turning away, Jody raced past the first line of campers toward a sprawling shed. One lightbulb over its open entrance dimly revealed a cavernous space within. An attached building, lower and more compact, had to be the showroom and office. Now he could see the fixed glass in front and a door with smaller windows to the right.

It was as though he had returned to his original time zone. He was no longer floating, no longer forcing his way through invisible pulp. He wondered which door was sure to be wired: this one leading from the inside of the huge shed to the showroom, or the outer door? There was no time for indecision. He bumped against the edge of the entry into the shed, and the hardness at his shoulder worked like a prod. Turning, he dashed around to the storefront, then slowed, walking upright, raising the bolt cutter to drag it against the side of the building and across the fixed glass pane.

There was still more he might do. Surely there was a better chance of tripping the alarm on the window at the end of the wall.

But finding it open brought him up short. Did open mean the alarm was disconnected? Not necessarily. The screen could be wired, too, allowing the window to be left open to let the night air cool off the office.

Jody ran his hand across the screen, then pressed as hard as he dared. If Phil was right, all Jody needed to do was make the sensor believe he was trying to jimmy it open. Not that anyone serious about breaking and entering would be stopped by a stupid screen.

"Jody!" The call was soft but urgent.

"Coming," he answered.

He still had to deposit Mom's envelope. He tried to insert it into the crack of the door, but the money made it too thick to be slipped in. Leaning against the door, he pushed with all his might until he could get the edge of the envelope stuck in the crack.

Then, after setting the bolt cutter on the ground, he ran back to the gate, where Mom and Aunt Marie held the muzzled dog. Its breaths rasped as if it were half strangled.

"Easy, boy," Mom was saying. "We'll have this off you in a second."

The van crossed the road and pulled up beside them.

"Everybody in," Phil declared from behind the wheel.

Jody's mother and aunt managed to lift and shove the big dog up into the van ahead of themselves.

"Okay," Phil said. "Jody, close the gate and get in."

Jody started to drag the gate and then stopped to exclaim, "The bolt cutter! I forgot it!"

"Get it," his mother told him. "Hurry."

"It's all the way back with the envelope," Jody said.

"Leave it, then," Marie said.

"No," Phil objected. "We can't wait, though. Brenda will have to come back for you."

"No," Jody's mother protested. "I'm not leaving him."

"We can't stay here with this dog," he told her. "I'll have you at your car in two minutes. Two more and you're back here." Mom got in the van, and Phil drove off.

Inside the lot again Jody finished closing the gate before going back to retrieve the bolt cutter. It was easier now that his fingers were working. It occurred to him that appearances like an open gate didn't really matter anymore, except maybe to show Phil that Jody had played by the rules. If Phil thought that Jody had just been clumsy and had tripped the alarm by accident, that could only reinforce the effect of the arrest. Phil wouldn't want Jody near any more rescues for a long time to come.

Everything was working, unless his mother returned before the police showed up. He hoped that Phil had exaggerated to make her feel better. It must take more than two minutes to get back to that liquor store, maybe five. There might be as much as a ten-minute period. Unless the alarm system had failed, Jody had to have set it off. There ought to be time enough for the police to come for him before his mother appeared.

Just to make sure, Jody dawdled around the building, pressing with his hands and scraping with the bolt cutter wherever there might be a sensor. Then he had to fight an impulse to run. He forced himself to walk, to stay cool.

He didn't have to pretend that the bolt cutter slowed his climbing. The tool was heavy and awkward to grasp because he needed both hands and feet to scale the fence. He had just dropped the bolt cutter over the top and was stretched full length on the fence when a police cruiser swung off the road. It stopped in front of the closed gate, but only for a second. Then the driver backed and angled the cruiser. Jody was caught in the glare of its high beams.

He knew that he should be elated, but his heart was racing. It was crazy to feel so scared when this was exactly what he had planned. The timing was perfect. Now when his mother drove back, she would see what was happening and steer clear of this place. The sooner she got herself home, the sooner the police would be able to reach her about her delinquent son.

The officer asked Jody whether he was alone.

Jody thought the answer was pretty obvious, but he tried to speak politely. "No one else is here with me." To his surprise, he found that his mouth had gone dry. It was hard to get the words out.

"Come down," the officer told him.

Jody had snagged his sneaker on one of the prongs of a broken link. "Just a minute," he said as he tried to kick free. He had to climb backward. It felt weird being strung up like this. The high-beam lights seemed to impale him.

But when he finally swung his leg over the top, he was able to see above the lights to the road. Was that Mom coming along, braking? It had to be. Fine. There was nothing suspicious about a passing car slowing down to watch an arrest in progress. Good, now the car was picking up speed. Everything was working out. He dropped to the ground.

The police officer was questioning Jody right in front of the lights when a second cruiser pulled in beside the first. This officer stepped back to speak to the driver. At the same time another set of lights appeared. Three cruisers? This was beginning to feel like overkill. What were those guys looking for?

Jody could only hear a few disjointed words like "juvenile" and "prank." Then the arresting officer spoke from the darkness: "You're a long way from home, aren't you? How'd you get here?"

Before Jody could think of an answer, his mother shouted, "I brought him. I put him up to it." So the third set of headlights belonged to Mom's car. What was she doing? Couldn't she see this was a bust?

"Up to what? Who are you?"

Jody was aghast. Mom wasn't supposed to stop like this. The drill was to separate herself from whatever they caught him doing and later pose as an indignant mother who never imagined her son getting into trouble.

Only here she was, identifying herself, producing her driver's license, and saying almost eagerly, "I'll explain. I can explain."

The officer called in to the dispatcher. Mom kept on talking as if she couldn't stop. The driver directed Jody into the cruiser.

"What about my mother?" Jody asked when the door was slammed. He needed to hear what she said so that he wouldn't contradict her.

"She'll be along," the officer told him.

Feeling baffled and deflated, Jody sank back. Why had Mom turned herself in? Did she think he couldn't handle being arrested? It had happened before, sort of. And as long as he was under fourteen, it wasn't all that hard for her to get him out of this kind of mess. But how was she herself going to get sprung? How long would it take? And what about the guard dog that needed treatment?

Jody was glad that the officer didn't speak to him. The radio voice that blatted on and off sounded like every cop show on television. Jody could ignore it as easily as if he were slouched in front of the screen. He had to collect his thoughts. If he let what had happened here throw him, he could lose whatever advantage he had gained for Moss. But he kept stumbling over this crazy turn of events. How could he have guessed that it would be Mom who refused to play the game? And how would it affect his plan?

At the police station everyone was surprisingly nice to him. He used the bathroom and then munched on some peanut butter and cheese crackers that the dispatcher gave him. When a police-woman saw that he was listening to a report that he guessed was about his break-in, she took him into another room. The last thing he heard before the door closed was that his mother had no priors. He had a feeling that the officers on duty thought the situation was pretty weird.

So his mother was definitely out of commission for a while, too. He had been aiming for something less drastic through his own arrest, but the result was likely to be the same where Moss was concerned. With or without the guard dog, no one, especially Mom, could afford to have Moss anywhere on the premises, since there was a good chance some police or social service person would be investigating Jody's home setup. That was what Jody had been counting on. The downside was that now that Mom had turned herself in, she couldn't take any chances at all, like bringing Moss to a sheepdog trial.

At least Jody had begun to pave the way for help from Dad and Sharon. Still, any Thelma-and-Louise type of "rescue mis-sion" would be a sore subject with Dad. Jody had planned to skirt around it. He'd figured Mom wouldn't want Dad to get wind of Jody's arrest. Once he got himself caught, she would probably take any help she could get to have Moss safely removed. She would be grateful to Jody for Dad's assistance. If Dad agreed to help.

But if Dad found out what had gone down tonight, everything Jody had depended on could be changed.

Changed how? he wondered.

Look on the bright side, he reminded himself. Which was? Well, for starters, if Mom couldn't take him and herself home soon, probably she would call Aunt Marie. The last thing Aunt Marie would do was tell Dad. But Mom was needed to work on that guard dog. Probably Marie was already on her way here. Any minute now the door would open, and there they would both be, Thelma and Louise, telling Jody to get a move on.

32 Jody woke up slumped over a table, his arm shielding his face from the overhead light. He was still dreaming that he was in some prison where they kept you awake to break you. His torturers were automotive robots with high-beam eyes he could not escape.

Even after hands propped him upright in the chair, he tried to fling himself face forward onto the table again.

"He's beat," someone said.

Beaten, thought Jody. No wonder his shoulders and neck were so sore. His whole body ached. If only they would tell him what to confess. If only he knew what they had got out of Mom.

Mom! He looked up. Here was a different police officer. Here was Jody's father.

"Come on," said Dad. "We both need our sleep."

Jody squinted at his hands and then tried to rub off the red welts that crisscrossed his palms.

"Time to go home," said the police officer.

"Where's Mom?" Jody asked. If he wasn't dreaming, then she ought to be here.

"In the slammer," said his dad. "Let's get out of here."

"Without her?" Jody rose and then clutched the edge of the table.

"She called me. She wants me to take you home for now."

Jody walked unsteadily into the outer room. Already that image of cars grilling him was fading. An officer ripped a sheet of paper from a pad and handed it to Jody's father. The dispatcher nodded at him and said, "Good luck." Then he looked at Jody. "Okay, son. You mind your dad."

It wasn't exactly dark out anymore. Jody said, "Is it morning?" Warming to the thought, he added, "Did I spend the night in jail?" Then he remembered about his mother and asked why she wasn't released, too.

"We'll talk about it later. After you get some sleep and I drink a gallon of coffee so I can stay at work today." Dad sounded ripped.

But during the drive home Jody suddenly clenched up. "Where is she?" he blurted. "Where's Mom?"

"I told you," said his Dad. "She has to be in court tomorrow. She's pleading guilty. She'll probably be let go."

"Guilty?" Jody exclaimed. "What did she do?" He meant: What did she say she did? He was fully awake now. It was important for him to know what she had confessed.

Dad glanced at him. "You don't know?"

"Oh, right, yeah." Jody was stumped. He wasn't supposed to talk about this stuff, especially with Dad. But what if he had to testify or something? After a moment he asked, "Will there be like a trial?"

Dad shook his head. "The judge will just sentence her, that's all." Then as an afterthought he said, "She might not even be fined since she already left money for the fence."

"How did you know she did that?" Jody exclaimed.

Again Dad threw a quick glance his way. "The police told me. They were joking about it when I came in. Said Brenda did more than turn herself in. It was like she turned herself inside out to take all the blame."

Jody heaved a sigh. He had heard enough to understand that

Mom mustn't have pretended attempted robbery. If the police had the money, then they had the printout about dog abuse that was in the same envelope. Only then did it occur to him that if the police knew that much, they would go after the guard dog. "Won't they make her tell where the dog is?" he asked.

Since they were stopped at a red light, the look Dad cast at Jody lingered a moment. Then he asked, "How come you don't know the police have the dog?"

"I—they took me away." Jody was plunged into confusion. Was it possible that Dad was tricking him? If the police had the guard dog, that would mean they had Phil and Aunt Marie as well. But Dad hadn't mentioned them.

Then it struck Jody like a physical blow. They had shifted the dog from the van to Mom's car. That's why it had taken her so long to get back to him. Phil and Aunt Marie were out of it, home free. Mom was taking the heat for all of them. "So what happened to the dog?" he had to ask. If the owner got it back, then the mission was a dead loss.

"Animal control has the dog. They're going to investigate conditions where it was kept. Could be Brenda's more effective landing herself in jail than anything else."

Jody guessed Dad was teasing now. Did that mean he was getting over being mad about all of this? Had Sharon had a chance to mention this coming weekend? If she hadn't, would Dad need a cooling-off period before he could be approached about the sheepdog trial? Jody guessed he better make himself invisible until Dad had caught up on sleep and was back in his usual routine.

Becoming invisible wouldn't be so easy, Jody realized as soon as Sharon opened the front door. Clearly she had been waiting anxiously for them.

Jody dropped to his knees to hug Moss, who came slinking over with his tail pressed to his belly. His cringing manner made it clear that he regarded this nightlong abandonment as some sort of punishment. He refused to look Jody in the eye but simply ducked his head against Jody's chest and leaned into him.

"What's the matter with the dog?" Dad demanded irritably.

Sharon shrugged. "Dogs get notions," she said. "Especially this one."

Moss stuck to Jody like Velcro, even when he went to take a shower. By then Jody was so out of it that he realized only after taking Moss for a quick pee that he had gone out wearing nothing but his father's underwear.

Fortunately Sharon and Dad were in the kitchen, Sharon making breakfast while Dad filled her in on the night's events.

Heading for the living room sofa that Sharon had made up for him, Jody thought it might be a good idea to hear Dad's take on the arrest. But the moment Jody's head hit the pillow, he felt himself diving into the deepest sleep of his life. He tugged just once at the sheet, and then his hand dropped heavily to the floor. Not to the floor. On Moss, who pressed against the sofa in unrestful stillness, taking no chances.

33 When Jody got up around noon, he found a stack of clothes from home. His dad was gone, and Sharon was in the kitchen with a hairdressing client. She came into the living room with a muffin and a glass of milk and asked him if that could hold him until the kitchen was free. He said it was fine. He asked about his clothes, and she told him Marie had dropped them off on her way to work.

"What about Mom?" he asked.

"You'll probably hear from her later today. If she gets out by noon, she plans to go straight to the animal hospital. Why don't you take the dog out now? Give me another hour or so, and I'll fix you something to eat."

But Jody had to know whether Sharon had spoken to Dad yet about the weekend.

"There wasn't much to say since you didn't tell me what you've got in mind," Sharon pointed out. "But if it has to do with the dog, which I assume it does, I didn't need to pave the way. The dog took care of your dad himself."

What was she getting at?

Sharon, already turning back to the kitchen, said, "Your father saw the two of you sleeping like long-lost buddies. He's hooked."

It was too hot at midday to go as far as the park or the high school, so Jody just walked Moss around the neighborhood to kill the next hour. He knew he ought to have a clear proposal ready for his father, but every time he started to work out a strategy, he was reminded of last night. No matter how carefully you planned, unexpected things could happen.

He figured it would be easier if Janet weren't at the Chiswick trial. Probably any number of handlers could tell him her last name and where she lived. Then all they would have to do was find that place, wait until dark, and tie Moss somewhere close to Janet's house or barn. They could even call her from somewhere nearby. By the time she began to wonder who had dognapped him, they would be long gone.

Still, Jody couldn't help hoping that Janet would be at the fair. If he could hitch Moss to her van without being observed, that would be pretty simple. The time to do it would be when she ran her dog. But even then someone else might be around and see.

His alternative plan also depended on perfect timing. It was trickier to put over, but it could work, and it might even allow him a glimpse of the reunion.

He was glad now that he hadn't spelled out all this to his mother when he thought he might win her over. The less she knew about what he had to do, the easier it would be for her to deal with Aunt Marie and Phil.

Not that Jody cared all that much about easing any strain in her relationship with Phil. He hated that she wouldn't stand up to him when she thought he was wrong.

Or had she changed? What was she up to last night when she turned back to bail out Jody? It had certainly put her out of the rescue business, at least for a while.

When all this was over, Jody thought, he would make sure that he didn't get tangled up with these games adults played. Playing by the rules was a laugh. Who did Phil think he was kidding? As far as Jody could see, adults had their own set of rules or made them up as they went along.

He looked down at Moss, who trotted beside him without glancing right or left, incurious, cut off from all that gave his life meaning and purpose. It seemed natural to Jody that they connected. A dog person might think that this was because Jody exercised and fed Moss. But it was more like a connection between equals, as if Moss could sense what Jody had been striving for all these weeks together.

That evening, when Jody came out with his proposal, his father seemed at first surprised. "It's not what I'd've guessed," he said. "I thought maybe you were going to see if there was a way you could keep the dog. Not that you were looking for his owner."

Jody shook his head. It occurred to him that Dad didn't know what was behind Moss's injuries. All Dad knew was that this dog had been found beside the road nearly dead and that Mom had rescued him. Jody said, "He needs to go home. It's all he wants. It's what I want."

"Maybe you'd like a dog of your own," Dad said. "Now that you've done so well with this one."

Jody shook his head again. "I don't much like dogs," he said.

"You could've fooled me," Dad told him. "This one looks like your buddy."

Jody nodded. "This one's different," he said.

The phone rang. Sharon answered it and said, "Which one do you want to speak to first?"

Jody jumped up and practically tore the receiver out of her hand. "Mom?" he shouted.

His mother replied in an undertone. "I'm calling from the animal hospital. I can't talk long. Are you doing all right? Lad okay?"

"Yes. What's going on? What happened anyway?"

"Well, it looks like that dog's saved. The owner's being cited. It's a long story, Jody. I think you ought to stay with your dad, at least until school starts. I'm going to be pretty busy for a while."

"What do you mean, busy?"

"I have to do community service. Sixty hours at an animal shelter."

"Sixty hours!" Jody exclaimed.

"Not all at once. Weekends and evenings. It could be worse. It's better than jail time, which would mean I'd lose my job. But I'll be tied up for a while. So I need to talk to your father."

"When will I see you?" Jody asked.

"Sunday, maybe. Let me talk to Dad."

"Okay."

"One more thing, Jody. Marie and Phil think we were together when the police came. You understand?"

Jody nodded.

"Jody? Did you say anything different?"

"No. I didn't say anything at all."

"Good." Mom sounded relieved. "Oh, good. Put your father on now. I'll talk to you tomorrow."

Jody was so absorbed by what she had revealed to him that he didn't bother to listen to his father's side of the conversation. Only Jody and Mom knew that while he was being caught and she was still able to drive away, this time she hadn't played by the rules. Instead she had turned herself in. Did she guess that he had tripped the alarm? Would they ever be able to talk about it together?

"Well," said Dad after hanging up, "I guess we have something of an all-clear."

"You mean there's no follow-up with Jody?" Sharon asked him. "That's a relief. I wasn't looking forward to any official type nosing around here."

"No," Dad told her, "we're still due for a visit, but they're not going to be looking at your business setup. It's just required where a juvenile's involved."

But Sharon glowered. "What'll they be looking for?"

Dad shrugged. "Obvious stuff like drugs, I suppose. Abuse. That sort of thing."

She shook her head. "I don't like not knowing what to expect."

"So sue me. This is Brenda's mess, not mine. What do you want me to do about it? You were the one who wanted us to take the dog." He broke off. They both looked at Jody, as if just remembering he was there with them.

Jody stood up, walked into the living room, and turned on the television. He found a talk show and tried to focus on the woman who was about to meet her long-lost half sister. But as his father's and Sharon's voices rose, it was impossible to blot them out.

"They're attached," his father was saying. "It's a damn shame he can't just keep the dog now that he's begun to shape up. It's been the making of him."

"Ssh," Sharon warned.

"What?" Dad's voice grew louder. "What did I say? It's true. You know he'll go back to vegging out like before. The least Brenda can do is find him another dog to work out with."

"You still don't get it, do you?" Sharon came near to shouting. "You're talking about muscles. It's not the running that's made the difference; it's the loving. Do you have any idea how tough it is to hold out like he's done? Is doing," she amended. "Now go in there and tell him we're behind him."

Absolute silence followed this tirade. Applause from the television audience welled up around Jody. It was still going strong when his father came in to anounce that they'd go along with Jody's plan. If they needed to be at that fair the day after tomorrow, it would mean an early start.

Jody nodded. Dad didn't have to worry about his being ready. He already was. He didn't think he'd be getting much sleep, if any, until Saturday had come and gone.

34 Jody spent Friday trying to run himself into the ground. Even though the playground was a lot farther from his father's house, he made it part of his route. If he and Moss spent part of this last day with Tara, he knew he would feel better about not telling her that this was the last time she and the kids would see Moss. But when Tara didn't show, Jody had to move on.

He ended up at the high school track, where he was able to keep on running until Sam called him out for a cross-country race. For a while it almost looked as though Jody were going to win. But then he became aware of Moss's limp, which was more pronounced than usual, so he slowed down. Jody didn't mind losing again. If things went as he hoped, soon he would be free to run against Sam without anything holding him back. While he nodded automatically when Sam urged him to get some decent running shoes, Jody kept his eye on the dog's game fore-leg. After tomorrow Moss wouldn't have to run on asphalt ever again.

Saturday morning in the pickup Jody kept glancing down at Moss. This was the last time he would feel the dog pressed against his legs like this. Jody kept his hands to himself, though. Moss leaning on him like this was all the contact Jody needed.

The farther north they went, the darker it grew. They drove through a cloudburst and then into bright sunshine. As they pulled off the highway, the countryside looked washed and renewed. The air felt cooler and cleaner.

Jody asked if they could give Moss a pee break before they got to the fair. Since he didn't know what the parking would be like or how long they would have to wait before getting Moss out, he wanted to make sure the dog was comfortable.

Dad stopped at a rest area, stretched, and leaned back for a catnap. Sharon came out with Jody to stretch her legs. Moss sniffed and lifted his leg and then sat down.

Sharon said, "You know, Jody, this may be tougher on you than you bargained for."

He said, "I've been getting ready for such a long time, it's like it's already happened."

"Still . . ." She fell silent for a moment. Then she added, "Finishing may be harder than getting yourself busted. That's all."

Jody whipped around. "How did you know—" He broke off.

"It's all right. Maybe your mother's guessed by now, but I don't think anyone else knows."

"I didn't think it would be that obvious," he said.

Sharon shook her head. "It wasn't. But remember when you first asked me about taking the dog if he was in danger? That kind of tipped me off that you were up to something, though I had no idea what. Then after the police called in the middle of the night and your dad left to get you, I figured out that you must've been planning the bust. You were afraid of what the others might do with Moss, weren't you?"

Nodding, Jody felt the heat rise in his face. "See, that's what worries me about today. I never thought Mom would get herself busted, too. I make dumb mistakes."

"Not dumb," said Sharon. "You can't expect everything to go like clockwork. Anyhow, you're not all by yourself here."

"So is it okay if I need you to keep Moss out of sight while I check things out?"

"Of course. And as long as your dad can't get in trouble, he'll help, too."

Jody wasn't so sure about that, but at least if one of them

could hold on to Moss, he wouldn't have to be left in the hot cab.

As it turned out, though, Moss stuck his head up at the window just as they came through the fair gate, and the ticket seller waved on Jody's father and yelled ahead to a parking person that this truck was to be allowed through to the sheepdog trial.

By now Moss was standing on Jody's lap and straining out the window.

"He must've been here before," Dad said.

"Don't get too close to those campers," Jody warned.

"Where do you want me to go?" Dad asked.

Jody was so mashed under the dog that he couldn't see much on either side.

"How about that way?" Sharon suggested.

"I don't know," Jody said.

"We'll try it," Dad decided. "Horses," he said. "Trotters. See, this is the end of a racetrack. These are horse stalls. You wait here. Sharon and I can have a look around." He stopped the truck in front of a paddock.

"What if someone comes?" Jody asked.

"Tell the truth," Dad answered. "Say you're waiting for your father."

As soon as he and Sharon got out, Moss moved across the seat and leaned out the open window. Jody kept a firm grip on the leash.

It seemed an eternity before Dad and Sharon returned. Jody had been right to steer clear of the campers. All the vehicles lined up there had sheepdogs tied to them. The trial course was on the infield of the racetrack. There were about sixty dogs entered. Nearly twenty had already run. The announcer said they hoped to get another ten runs in before they broke for lunch.

"We watched a couple of dogs working the sheep," Sharon said. "They're amazing."

"So how about it?" said Dad. "Want to have a look around the fair? There's lots of other things going on."

Jody shook his head. "Are there many people watching?" How big a crowd did he need to get Moss close without being noticed? "Could you go back and see if there's someone named Janet listed? Her dog's name would be there, too. Tess."

"You couldn't think to tell us that before?"

"I thought I could find out myself. Now I'm not so sure I should be there ahead of time. Someone might recognize me."

"So what?" Dad told him. "It's not a crime to watch a sheep-dog trial, is it?"

"Then will you stay here with Moss while I go look?"

Sharon said, "Why don't I walk the dog around behind the horse barn?"

Jody didn't know what to think or do. Everything seemed both normal and perilous at the same time. What if Moss got away from Sharon? In his excitement he might run off again. "Hold him tight," Jody said. "Really, really tight. See how he's trembling? He might not listen anymore. Even to me." Did he risk losing Moss if he let him out of his sight, even for a few minutes?

Jody veered back and forth, weighing risks and needs. But he couldn't bring off the return without seeing exactly where the gate to the trial course was and where the sheep pens were. He ought to walk around the area. If Janet was there, it would be important to know where her van was parked, how close it was to the entry gate.

So Jody left Moss with Sharon and Dad and promised to be back in about ten minutes. Starting at a run, he had to force himself to slow down, to blend in with the audience. He practiced sauntering as he approached the grandstand. That felt so phony it only made him self-conscious. The thing to do was worm his way through to the fence, watch the dog on course, and then move on.

It took awhile to locate the scoreboard, which was taped to the side of a van. Someone with a marker was copying scores from the judge's sheets onto the board. A few handlers were craning to see the numbers. Jody looked down the list of handlers still to run. Janet and Tess were near the bottom, number forty-seven. He whipped around, nearly colliding with Diane, who said, "Sorry," and "Oh, hi." She started around the back of the van before full recognition hit. Then she stopped. "Hi!" His name followed after a pause. "Jody. Jody, right?"

He nodded. He was nailed.

"I almost didn't—" She broke off. "You look different."

He said. "You look the same." He knew at once that they could pick up right where they had left off. It would be easy to talk to Diane and not talk, both.

"Zanna's here," she said. "You know, my friend," she added. "The one that owns Moss. We still keep hoping he'll show up. Janet says there's a chance because everyone searched and searched, and there were no, you know, like remains. But it's awful not knowing."

Jody opened his mouth, but no words came. Lies would be unbearable. Finally he said, "I thought about you a lot, about what you were going through. I wanted to stay and help look for him."

"They never did figure out how it all started, the gate left open and all. You going to be here for the whole trial?"

He shook his head. "Only for a while."

"Well, I'll see you," she said. "I'm supposed to take a message down to the guy in the holding pen. We'll be around all day."

As soon as she left, Jody strolled behind the tied dogs until he came to what he was pretty sure was the rear of Janet's van. The dog hitched to it was a black and white Border Collie that looked like most of the others. Anyway, he didn't expect to recognize Tess. What mattered, though, was that there were three trucks, one car, and one motor home between this van and the handler's gate onto the course. That seemed more than enough of a visual barrier. The grandstand was just beyond the gate in the other direction. All Sharon and Dad needed to do was position themselves and Moss between the grandstand and the fence so that Jody could move swiftly once he took Moss from them.

He went there to check out distances and timing. Turning, he tried to scan the tiers of men seated in the audience. If he could identify the forklift driver, he had a better chance of avoiding him. The last thing he needed was to run in to him the way he had run into Diane. The forklift driver was the one person who could place Moss with Jody at home.

But this entire end of the racetrack was surrounded by people crowding up to the fence. The forklift driver could be anywhere or nowhere. Jody had to take his chances about that. He needed to figure out how many more dogs were to run before the sheep would be driven back to the holding pen at the opposite end of the course. He needed to have Moss ready when all the sheep were out there.

35 They were too late. Neither Sharon nor Dad understood why the timing had to be so precise. True, Jody didn't give them much leeway. But that was only because he barely had time himself. From the moment he realized there were only three runs to go before the sheep would be moved, he had to get back to the horse barns, instruct Sharon and Dad about keeping Moss right between them, and then explain exactly where they must stand. Exactly.

Dad reacted to Jody's telling him what he should do by questioning Jody's plan and challenging his judgment.

"We don't have time for this!" Jody exclaimed.

Dad said, "Well, if you think I'm going to walk into some kind of booby trap—"

And Sharon told them both to cool it. "You're innocent," she reminded Jody's father. "Even if they connect you and the dog, you don't have to take the heat for Brenda. So let's just get this over with."

Jody raced ahead of them. He wanted to be there and dogless until the last possible second. But when the sheep were let out of the exhaust pen, Dad and Sharon were only just ambling up to the grandstand. Unless Jody ran to meet them and snatched Moss in plain sight of just about everybody, the sheep would be across the course and closed into the holding pen before Jody could slip Moss inside the gate.

Jody was so disappointed, so discouraged that he almost gave up. He felt like walking right up to Janet's van and handing over the dog. And explaining everything. What kept him from doing that was his mother, knowing what she had done for him. And, he now understood, not just for him but for Moss, too. If Jody got caught here or gave himself up, it would be Mom who took the heat, just as Sharon had said.

So Jody waited until Sharon and Dad had finally positioned themselves, with Moss held tightly between them, all of them jammed between spectators standing in front of the grandstand, and then he sidled up to them and informed them that the opportunity had slipped by.

"How long do we have to wait?" Dad demanded.

Jody was about to suggest that they take Moss back to the horse barn area when the announcer declared over the loudspeaker that there would be a lunch break at twelve-thirty, the trial to resume a little after one o'clock. The announcer went on to name the handler on the course and the two to follow. After those runs, the announcer informed the audience and competitors, there would probably be time for two more dogs to run before the break.

"Just till twelve-thirty," Jody told his father. "They won't keep the sheep penned up." He spoke with more certainty than he felt, but he was afraid of Dad's wandering off.

Jody stooped down to Moss, who strained toward the sheep without actually moving, his muscles coiled as though to spring. "Hold on," Jody said softly. "I'll be back."

Jody stepped away and watched the next runs without really seeing them. He could almost sense how each dog was doing from the sharpness of the whistling or the tone of each handler's voice. In a few minutes Jody would issue his first and last sheep-handling command. Once Moss was enclosed on the trial course, it would hardly matter if he failed to respond the right way. But if he did, if just this once Jody could feel what it was like to send the dog to sheep, it would be a gift, a gift from Moss.

The waiting seemed endless. Then suddenly it was over. The time had come for Jody to make his move. The final competing dog of the morning brought the sheep out of the exhaust pen. The announcer blared through the public-address system that the sheep in the holding pen should be released to graze on the infield.

Since people in the grandstand stood up all at once, no one could make any headway. Those crowded at the fence were also clogged, all of them talking about what kind of food to head for. The announcer reminded everyone to return for the afternoon runs, and in the midst of all this noise and confusion, Jody pushed through to Moss. There he waited for the last dog and its handler to leave.

At the far end of the course sheep streamed out of the holding pen and spread out, heads already down to the grass. Jody led Moss through the gate and knelt beside him. "Moss, Moss." He spoke with his head touching the dog's, both his hands on the collar as he unbuckled it. "Moss," Jody repeated, holding the dog with his voice, dragging his attention for an instant from the two groups of sheep beyond them. Then, letting go, Jody said, "Look back! Look back, Moss!"

Moss leaped away. Swinging out toward the more distant sheep, he ran as wide as the fence allowed to circle behind them.

"Dog loose on the course!" the announcer shouted. "Handlers, one of your dogs is out there." After a moment a voice close to the announcer could be heard through the speakers: "That dog looks like the one that was lost. Call Janet."

Clutching the collar and leash, Jody slipped back through the gate to become a part of the crowd. But he couldn't leave yet, not while Moss was still gathering the sheep for him. He forced his way against the press of departing spectators until he could stand unnoticed at the fence.

"Janet, Janet," someone else shouted. "Come quick."

By the time Jody had a clear view onto the course, Moss had peeled off to bring the sheep from the exhaust pen together with the first group. Several people were running toward him, and one of them seemed to be calling. Jody was too far away to hear the words. But he saw Janet dash through the gate, two girls in her wake. He even heard her whistle and saw Moss drop to the ground.

Another softer whistle, and Moss rose and crept forward. He had gone out on a signal from Jody, but now he was responding to Janet. The shift in his focus was so slight it was nearly imperceptible. It was almost as if Janet had risen from the place where Jody had knelt with Moss before sending him to the sheep.

One more whistle, this one summoning the dog, confirmed the changeover. Jody noticed that Moss still favored his foreleg, but it didn't slow him. He moved with such fluid power that he seemed to ride a current that swept him toward his true, his ultimate shore. By now Janet and the girls were rushing headlong to meet him.

All at once so many people surrounded Moss that Jody had only momentary glimpses. One was of Janet holding the dog, another of Moss on his back, of all things, with one girl practically smothering him and the other, Diane, her arms flung wide, her face tipped up, shouting to the skies.

He longed to stay. He knew he shouldn't. Probably Sharon and Dad were already in the truck and anxious to get going. Jody tried to tell himself that it couldn't hurt to see Moss one more time. But of course it could, because anyone who knew Moss would be able to feel the connection between them.

The horse barn was in sight before Jody realized he was still in possession of evidence: Moss's collar and leash. He looked around for a trash barrel and saw none. If he was leaving now, probably it didn't matter. Besides, who could say that it wouldn't come in handy one day if Mom decided to adopt some kind of shelter dog?

But the collar was steeped in Moss's scent. He supposed that eventually another dog might be able to wear it without noticing. Not yet, though. Just as it would be awhile before Moss's presence faded from all the places Jody must return to alone, it would take time for this collar to shed its Mossprint.

Jody paused. Only now that Moss was safe was it sinking in on him that there would be no Moss at the end of this day—or any other. Walking away from Moss involved more than slipping the collar and sending him to sheep. It meant losing him so that he could be found.

Jody drew a long breath. He had to remind himself that Moss was going home. Up ahead Dad and Sharon were waiting. It was time for Jody to go home, too.

Author's Note

Through time humankind's relationship with animals has undergone many changes, perhaps the most crucial being the transition from a subsistence economy based on hunting to animal husbandry. And even hunters and gatherers have lived with animals.

Sheepdogs have been essential to farmers and shepherds for a long time. No human can cover ground like a dog gathering far-ranging sheep from steep hillsides. Since the farmer strives to cause as little stress as possible to the livestock, Border Collies have been bred not only for endurance and swiftness but also for intelligence and sensitivity. Whether on the Scottish moors or in the plains or high country of the American West or on islands off the coast of Maine or Canada, a dog must be able to work at a great distance from its handler. The working partnership between human and dog and livestock takes time, patience, and trust as well as the right breeding.

Sheepdog trials originated in Great Britain when shepherds and sheep farmers got together to compare the herding prowess of their dogs. Trials replicate some of the maneuvers that are called for in handling livestock smoothly and efficiently, not only in large fields but also on tight courses more representative of barnyards and feedlots. While most Border Collies love to work, some prefer the farm or ranch to competing in public. A wise handler learns to respect that preference. It is only one of many things that attentive handlers learn from their dogs.

Over the centuries there have been many instances, recorded and unrecorded, of cruelty to animals. More common, however, are habits of neglect and callousness that have been simply taken for granted. People's efforts to heighten society's awareness of animal exploitation have led to many reforms. But just as extreme abuse of animals still may occur, so can extreme and unreasonable actions in the name of animal rights. Often the real issues are many-sided and complicated. This book tells a story and does not attempt to portray any existing organization. The characters are just that: invented characters. The simple truth is that even after public attitudes change and reform follows, the question of individual conduct and responsibility will always remain.